THE CIVIL WAR

Written From Dream Memory

Book One in
The Drifter Series

Jeffrey L. Holt

THE CIVIL WAR

Written From Dream Memory

Book One in
The Drifter Series

Jeffrey L. Holt

ELEVATION PRESS
OF COLORADO

The Civil War
Written From Dream Memory

Book One in
The Drifter Series

by Jeffrey L. Holt

Second Edition Copyright © 2025 by Jeffrey L. Holt

For more information, please see *About the Author* at the close of this book and visit benjaminauthor.com

Front cover image: Author-Prompt/NightCafe Studio, 2025
Cover design and interior design and formatting by Donna Marie Benjamin of Elevation Press of Colorado.

Jeffrey L. Holt
P.O. Box 555
Naturita, CO 81422

Ordering information: Quantity sales. Special discounts are available on quantity purchases by book clubs, corporations, associations, and others. For details, contact the publisher at the address above.

ISBN 978-0-932624-37-6

1. Main category— [Alternative History] 2. Other categories— [Dystopian]—[Adventure]

ELEVATION PRESS
Cedaredge, Colorado
www.elevation-press-books.com

Acknowledgments

First, and foremost, I would have to thank Lois Frederick. She encouraged me to write my experiences.

Next, I would like to thank Cheri Ann Karpiak for helping me to proofread and put my story in print. Since she is a close friend, it is the "icing on the cake" for me.

Last, but certainly not least, is my wife Tammie. She never failed to answer all of my questions, while still maintaining a full-time job of her own.

The most credit goes to the men and boys from both sides who gave their lives in this war.

Sincerely,
Jeff Holt

Preface

This story was written from dreams I had after taking a horseback tour of the Gettysburg, Pennsylvania, battlefield. I went through a long series of intense dreams during which I woke up gagging on what I imagined was cannon smoke and the smell of blood. It took several years to put all the dreams together and make sense of how they were connected to me. Of course, this has to be called fiction, but it was so real to me. I have a total of 25 years in this writing.

A big "thank you" to Don and Donna Marie Benjamin of Elevation Press of Colorado for pulling up their bootstraps and getting this project on the road.

CHAPTER 1

Civil War

These are memories and dreams of the Civil War. It was 1858, and everyone was upset and talking about the chances of this war. A war about states' rights or more like the keeping of slaves. The southern states used slave labor to work their large plantations of cotton. That was their cash crop, and slaves were needed to do all the chores involved, which included planting, picking and stuffing into large bags for shipment to the North. They were afraid that without slaves, they would have no crops to sell.

We lived in the North, halfway between Gettysburg and Philadelphia, Pennsylvania. On every trip into town, we could see posters asking for blacks to join the Northern Army and help free their Southern brothers and sisters.

Four of us boys and two girls, with our Ma and Pa, lived and worked on our 600-plus acres of good bottom ground. Pa always told us, when going into town, to just listen and never take sides. When we would get home, we would sit around the table after the supper dishes were cleared and talk about everything we had heard and seen.

My oldest brother, Walter, was near 21 years old and wanting to take on a wife. The next two boys, twins Andy and Andrew, were past 18 years old by two months. Then, the fourth boy in the family was me. I was 16 years old. The girls were Priscilla, age 14 years old, and Helen, age 12 years old.

Growing up, at times, I thought it was rather odd that Ma was the only one allowed to swear. When she talked to Pa, she called him "Doomis James." Not knowing that was Pa's proper name, I thought she was saying "Dumb Ass James." When I went to school, the teacher also called me Doomis. I never knew I was a Junior until just nine years ago.

Some of the family had left for the west but to hear Pa talk about them and the war, "They were running away." He continued, "We got no war with the south, we will stay put." Well, it played out differently. All us boys went to war. One never to return. Another one missing his arm. I came back to a burnt-down farm with no way to know where everyone went.

Ma's name was Kathleen and Pa called her Kathern, but her church friends and shops in town called her "Katy." Ma came from Bible people, and Pa came from the dirt. The boys were named by Pa. No real reason, or family connection, just a name he liked from somewhere. The boys were his department, and Ma took care of the girls and the girl things they needed.

My sister Priscilla was named after my mother's mother, and Helen after her dad's mother. It seemed to me that Priscilla had the only out-of-place name with that extra syllable. Now it comes to me, as I already mentioned, I imagined that my mother and some shop keepers called Pa "Dumb Ass James" whereas they called him "Doomis James." I was in my last year of school when it was explained to me that Pa's name was "Doomis James Lentz" and mine was "Doomis James Junior." Ma tacked the Junior on it for me. Anyhow, I have answered to "Dumb Ass" or "Junior" my whole life. My name on the Army roll call list was Doomis James Lentz, Jr. But I carried the nickname of Dumb Ass the rest of my life. Ninety percent of the people did not know my real name, and they were not upsetting me in the least.

I knew things were going to change soon. Every night, Pa and Walter would go to the woodshed to talk. When any of us asked about it, we were told "You'll know in due time." I never had a clue what they were talking about until the whole plan was laid out.

We had started helping our neighbor, old "Grampa Yoder" when he had close to 500 acres with no help. His four girls had moved away, leaving him and his wife on the farm. We helped as much as we could. Pa always tried to keep ahead of everything like big jobs that included plowing and putting up hay. We would take to Yoder's our two big teams of horses we used for logging, planting and anything else heavy. We worked our two light teams as well, because they were in good shape and they could do a lot of work.

We would bring them over in the evening when it was cool. It was close to six miles by way of the road, so we would need to rest them a couple of times. We would take a two-seat buggy in the morning so that we did not lose a lot of the daylight hours.

We helped Mr. Yoder all we could, in trade for saw logs and firewood from his wood lot. Pa had a small sawmill and made furniture to sell. He made a lot of tables and chair sets and bedroom suites. These went to newly-weds and Pa had orders that took the whole winter.

One time Helen wanted to do outside work. Thinking it would be easier than cleaning house and cooking. She found out quickly it was not, and she went back into the house.

One evening in late summer after dishes were cleared away Pa said "I have to go to town early tomorrow. Walter will be in charge as always." He turned to Helen and said, "I know tomorrow is your birthday. If I have a few pennies left over, is there anything you want from town?"

"No, Pa," she said. "But I would like a chance to work outside with the boys."

Pa just said, "That will be up to Walt."

That ask by Helen was a surprise to us all, but nothing more was said.

Next morning after, I woke up to smell coffee and bacon frying. I sat up on the edge of the bed and started dressing. I was tucking in my shirt when I heard Pa's big team and wagon rattle out of the yard.

At breakfast, Priscilla was at the stove. When Helen showed up, she was wearing her outside clothes. No need to guess if Walt had chosen to let her help. Walt being the farm boss with Pa away, he told us all to divide up the regular farm chores and then we were going to butcher a hog and needed to set up things for that.

When the inside and outside chores was done, Walt said for Helen to take the small team and light wagon and get us a load of firewood.

"Hitch up the horses," he told her. "Then go to the wood lot and fill it up with firewood. Don't worry to cut anything, just load what you can lift and the boys will do the cuttin.'"

Helen was taking a long time getting the horses out, so I went to see. She was not able to get the harness on because she was too short. I helped her and she brought them out to the wagon which we had pushed out of the shed. Andy was at the gate so she could go right through to the wood lot.

Us boys started setting up the tables we would need for the slaughter. The last thing to come out of the shed was a very large iron pot. It was so big it took all four of us to carry. We had poles that were about ten-foot long standing in the corner just for the job. The poles were put through the bail ears on the pot and each one of us got on an end. We got it all balanced up and, at Walt's word, we lifted and started walking across the yard. Walt was easy to work for. He kept his eye on everyone.

Halfway across the yard, he knew us smaller boys were struggling with the load, so he said stop, put it down. He called a halt before one of us had to. After a short time, we all got ready and, again at Walt's word, we were off.

We set the heavy iron pot down in the fire circle. He had sent Helen with a team of horses and wagon to the wood lot to get a load of branches to cut into firewood for kindling. Knowing she would be coming back about then, he looked up and just said "gate," and we knew she was back with a load of limbs for the fire, and we had to open the gate for her. Walt showed Helen where to dump them, but she could not get the horses to back up. Walt never said a word; he just looked at one of us and nodded his head toward the wagon. We knew this meant "jump up there and help her." I got up there and got the wagon back and the rest of my brothers fussed around the back. They were tying a rope to the bottom limbs.

With another nod from Walt, I eased the team forward and the load all came off at once. Walt now stepped up to the wagon and told Helen to get one more load. Andrew had the gate open, so she was able to drive right through. We started chopping and sawing the first load and stacking it close to the fire. The small wood was laid and Walt sent me to the house for one match and a small cup of lamp oil. When I got back, he put those things aside and we were now pumping and hauling water to fill the pot.

Everyone took a turn on the pump and, when the pot was half full, Walt lit the wood using the lamp oil and my one match. The fire was burning well as we finished cutting more big wood up. Walt made a quick trip to the house, and when he came back, Helen was also back with a second load of big wood. This time she was able to back the team to the pile, and we off-loaded the same way as before. And my brothers started cutting and sawing as before.

Helen mostly handled the team on her own. I just walked beside her to help her understand what was going on at the back of the wagon. When it was time to off-load, I made certain sure she should let the team walk ahead slowly and be ready to stop them if any of the big wood hung up. Everything went fine and she was told to drive wagon to the shed and unhook.

"Take the horses to the barn," Walt told her. "But don't let them drink yet. Andy will go with you and settle the horses. Then I need you back here right away."

When Helen came out, Walt told her to get the box of tools we used for butchering. She had a time finding the box and, when she came back, we could see she was covered with mud.

At this point, we went to the house for a quick meal. Ma had cold meat and cheese, and bread and cider all laid out. Walt sat in Pa's chair at the head of the table. Not to take over his place but so he could keep an eye on the boiling pot. Once during our hurried lunch, Walt said "Andrew" and nodded his head toward the outside pot. No other word was spoken. Andrew knew he was to tend the fire. After lunch, I was sent for the light-weight chain, Andy was sent for a bucket of feed, and Helen was sent to go unharness the team and give them water. Then a good brushing and check their feet to see if they had any stones stuck or if they had lost a shoe.

We all went outside but Walt. When he came out, he was carrying Pa's old rifle, cleaned real well.

There was an old stump in the corner of the hog yard and, at a nod from Walt, Andy poured the feed on it and just fussed around putting out more feed until the right hog was eating. Walt stepped up and put the gun behind its ear and fired one shot. The hog went down, and Walt handed the gun to Andy as he stepped over the fence to cut its throat.

We had put the first table near the hog fence and laid an old canvas tarp between the fence and the table. While Andrew made sure the other hogs stayed put, Walt called for the chain, and he put it through the hog's mouth. When he said "everybody," we knew to grab on to the chain and pull the hog out onto the canvas and out of the yard and over to the first table. At this point, Walt climbed up on the table and took the chain. We all just grabbed ahold and hefted the animal up.

When the dead hog was balanced on the edge, a tub was pushed under and Andy opened his belly, being careful not to cut too deep. As the guts came out, they all dropped into the tub. Without looking, Walt just said "lungs." Andy reached up into the rib cage and cut them and the heart loose. My brother was just out of the way when I threw a couple buckets of water up into the hog to wash him out. Now we all grabbed on and finished putting him up on the table. Walt said the water's not hot enough yet.

At this point, I went around the shed to pee and when I came back, Pa's big team and wagon was tied at the rail. I headed for it, but Walt said, "Helen can do it." He said, "Let's try this hog."

This meant we should slide the hog down into the boiling pot of water. Walt pulled out his pocket watch to check the time. It was the only time I seen him with it, except on Sundays. At the five-minute mark, we pulled him up on a table that was set up to drain the water back into the pot. We all started-in with bell scrapers, but soon found he needed another five in the water.

At this point, I ran to the barn, I knew my sister would have trouble putting the harness up on their hooks. She had them off and piled against the wall. I knew there would be words from Pa if the tack was left there, so I grabbed them up. As I ran out, I grabbed a pitchfork. When I got back to the fire, Walt took it and started pushing the hog underwater. Just like we had it planned.

This time, when we brought the hog out, he was ready to be scraped. Walt told everyone to grab a scraper. Helen came back but was lost at this. But she jumped right in and soon had hog hair all over the front of her. We scraped all we could, and the hog went back in the pot. This time for eight minutes. We just about got all the hair scraped this time. Then he went in for another eight-minute bath.

We finished scraping and Walt had the gambrel hook we used to hang hogs up to skin out. He had also got the tarp we would put under it again, this time to slide the hog on its way to the root cellar overhang. Using the tarp, we had to push, pull, drag him over without getting him on the ground. That was a little hard, but we managed.

When we reached the root cellar, Andy had the sharp knives out and trimmed back the hocks so we could hang him up. At this point, Helen was sent to the house to get the old bed sheets we used to cover anything we hung up. This kept the flys off. When Helen got inside, Ma had the sheets all stacked on the table. She had seen many animals butchered and knew we would want them sooner or later. While Helen was gone, I went for some wrapping twine. We used it to tie the sheets on.

Helen and me got back about the same time and Walt said the hog flesh was still too warm, and we would have to wait. About then, Pa came out of the house and headed across the yard. Walt met him halfway. Being my brother was in charge, he was reporting in.

The report must have not of been too much because they barely stopped. Then the two of them came back to where the rest of us waited. When Pa looked over the hog he said, "Looks good."

Then Pa said, "Why don't you boys clean barn a little and see to your night chores. Helen can watch the hog."

Seeing Helen covered in mud and hog hair he smiled. Then he told her to get a little switch to keep the flys and dogs away.

We all got busy with our chores, including Walt since Pa was back in charge. Just before supper Pa told us to wrap that hog before we went in. Wrapping was not hard once we got started. We had small slivers of wood to pin the sheets to and then tied everything with the twine. At this point we went to the house. We were done for the day. I didn't know it then, but this would be the last work we would do together as a family.

There was a package on the kitchen table also wrapped in cloth and tied with twine. We all knew that had to be Helen's gift even though she never asked Pa for one.

The next morning, Helen showed up at the table with her inside clothes on and wearing a new-bought fancy apron. Nothing was ever said about her working outside again.

Me and my brothers and sisters knew Walt was planning to marry soon. We could tell this by the amount of extra stock we were feeding. It was safe to say that added livestock was for setting up a new farm.

As war talk became more and more heated, Ma, Pa, and Walter set us all around the kitchen table one evening and laid out what all this secret wood-shed talk was about. Walt and Mr. Yoder's granddaughter, Catherine, were planning to marry. Everything was set up for them to take over his farm. The wedding was not talked about until a couple of months out. Walt's plan was to join the Army for a 14-month service, and then he would not get drafted. They would marry when he got back.

That explained all the extra stock we had been feeding and the land and rocks we cleared to make a road we brought out through Yoder's woods and our field. That new road would save two hours on a trip over to Yoder's farm.

CHAPTER 2

Joining the Service

In the spring of 1860, we all watched Walt board a train just outside of York. None of us would ever believe this would be our last look at him.

He was sent somewhere east and north of Boston. They were all off-loaded and sworn in. In less than 20 minutes, they were sworn in, checked by a doctor, showered and given new blue-coated uniforms with six big eagle-carved brass buttons.

His first letter home was short and told about getting up at 5:45 am to take a headcount, wash their face and hands and go to breakfast. At 7:00 am they made their bed, got their gear and formed up to do marching and drilling until their turn to eat at about 6:00 pm. Then it was eat, shower, in bed by 8:00 pm, and asleep by 8:30 pm.

His next letter told of drilling every day and one day a week they went to rifle range.

He wrote that they added the rest of the men to fill out their 100-man unit. He said he heard of talk that they were being sent to guard ammunition at the arsenal at Harper's Ferry, West Virginia.

His last letter came in February of 1861. They were told to "thin their gear" which meant throwing out everything not needed because they were shipping out in the morning to Fort Sumter. That was the last we ever heard from Walter. We have come to believe he was one of the men buried in the mass grave there.

Pa bought Mr. Yoder's farm and Catherine moved into the house with
our family and we farmed the land. She always hoped Walter would come
back, but it never happened.

Andy and Andrew were just boiling over with hate for the war, but they
wanted to do their part and also look for Walt. After joining the Army, they
went east and ended up north of Washington. Their letters home told the
same stories as Walt had done. They were up by 6:00 am, ate, and be ready
to drill all day by 7:00 am. Andy said they would drill until the "Big dog
wanted to stop," drill, drill, drill. Andrew said they were given an Enfield
rifle. They shot the new "Mini Ball." It had grooves in it, so it flew straighter
and tore flesh and bone when it went through. It had a long bayonet to poke
the enemy if they got too close. Andy was left-handed. He had a devil of a
time because things worked from the wrong side for him. Learning it took
him about two months.

The brothers were split up and Andrew stayed with his group and Andy
moved to a group who fired cannons all day. Since he was left-handed, he
could do so much more to help out with the heavy guns. When the cannon
was fired, his job was to swab the barrel with a wet mop to get the hot cin-
ders out. Then he would put a pre-wrapped powder charge down the barrel
and turn the mop around and push it down and give it one good thump to
seat it in. When he stepped aside another guy put a 12-pound ball in. Then
someone would light it off, and the whole cycle would start over again.

While Andy served with the cannon crew, Andrew was a flat-shoe soldier, which meant *drill, drill, drill* all day. When not drilling or sleeping,
they were on the rifle range. Someone was shot in the back as he tried to
get to his targets. Andy and Andrew remained split up and did not see each
other the rest of the war. Every time Andrew heard cannon fire, he would
tell everyone, "That's my brother." Of course, he had no way of knowing it
or not.

Chapter 3

Andy is Sent Home

Time seemed to go by so fast. We were short-handed on the farm, so Pa built a bunk house and hired farmhands, or "loafers" as Ma called them. On any day, there were men and boys hanging around the feed store. Some were so desperate that they would eat only half their evening meal and try to sneak the rest under their shirts to take home to their families.

Finally, Ma told them, "Might as well bring them along, if we got to feed them, might as well get a little work out them!"

That's how life was at our house from 1862 to 1865. Men who were desperate to feed their families came by every day. Some were alone, and some pitched tents in the grove of trees across the road. They even helped with a night watch and we soon stopped losing chickens and little pigs to thieves.

By 1863, I could not hold out any longer and I decided I had to sign up for the Army. I would sign up the following year and leave from the same town as everyone before me. There were many things that swayed my decision to enlist. We got a letter from Andy's commanding officer. My brother had received some sort of injury and was back at the hospital north of Washington. His letter said just that he had been injured at a field camp, or a hill above the Rappahannah River Bridge. He would be sent home to recuperate soon.

Pa got a telegram from the state department that said Andy would be here on the 3100 westbound on Friday. That gave Ma and the girls just two days to wash up his blankets and fix a big dinner. And it gave me time to see Andy before I would have to sign up.

Ma's jobs were all a lot easier in those days, with extra people to help, including Catherine and others. They set up the drain pot, made a good fire, and then poured one bucket of water in. With a long pole, they set it on the fire. One man and a boy carried wood while someone cut a bar of homemade soap into flakes. When the water came to a boil, the soap was put in and the whole mess was stirred with a long handled wooden spoon.

When the water was boiling, the blankets were put in and stirred. Ma said 30 minutes would be long enough for blankets. A second pot was filled with clean water which was brought to a boil and used to rinse the soap out. The blankets were pulled across a drain and twisted to get the rinse water out and then to the line to dry. The main pot was refilled from the rinse pot. That way water would be hot, and some soap would be returned to the wash water.

White and soft colors were washed first along with any of the "girls' under-things," working their way through socks, shirts, and work pants and coats that need washing. Everything was sorted out in a basket. I never knew my mother had so many baskets. Doing the wash still lasted all day, but there were a lot more hands to help.

At four o'clock the day Andy was coming home, it was bright from a full moon with cool air. Pa and I headed for the train and did not want to be late. We had two or three little stops to make, but I think they could have been taken care of another day. I think Pa just wanted to brag to everyone that one of his sons was coming home.

As we stepped out of the General Store, we heard the train whistle blow at the lower crossing. We just had enough time to get there before the train. We were standing on the platform when everyone started getting off. Near the end of this line was a guy helping an old lady off. Just like Andy, always helping someone.

My brother spotted Pa and me the same time that we did him. He had a large coat over his left arm and was helping the lady with his right arm. We never knew anything was wrong until Pa tried to hug my brother and Andy pulled back from the pain. Pa looked at me and we both looked at him as his topcoat slid to the ground. That's when we saw his left arm, from the elbow down, was gone. We just stood and stared. We could not say anything, and we did not know what to say.

Andy broke the silence. He looked at us and said, "Cannon misfired."

Then we just stayed there on the platform and hugged each other as we cried tears of happiness and sadness at the same time.

It was a long, quiet ride home. Pa was looking straight ahead and me never wanting to make eye contact with Andy. When we swung into the yard, Ma and the girls came running out. Like us, they did not see Andy's left arm. He got out of the wagon and the way he was standing by the back of the wagon hid his left arm while he waited for me to hand down his stuff.

Ma just couldn't wait, and she grabbed Andy in a big hug which is when she found out just like me and Pa did. Like us, she had to accept that his left arm and hand were gone. Everybody had a good welcome-home cry, and then everybody asked, "When do we eat?"

Ma had fixed Andy's favorites, roast chicken, corn on the cob, fresh bread and bread and butter pickles, grandma's coleslaw and cold beets. It was all washed down with all the sweet tea we could drink and fresh apple pie for dessert.

Andy was sat to the right of Pa, in Walt's old spot. Ma was on Pa's left so she could get to the stove quickly. That day Ma never got up, though. To wait on us, she had the help of my sisters who served as our family "waiters."

After we all ate our fill, no one left the table. We all knew Andy would eventually tell us about his arm. Andy cleared his throat and started to talk. He told us about being rolled out at 5:45 and 6:00 am. He told how every morning the Army made him line up for headcount and nobody could go to breakfast until all were accounted for. He said they had two or three guys who headed to the outhouse as soon as they got up, and every morning everybody else had to wait on them.

"After a couple of weeks," he said, "someone was put in charge of us while we were in the barracks. They got wise quick and made us all sleep close together and put an end to using the outhouse so early. Then we were rolled out 15 minutes ahead of everyone else."

Andy told jokes on different guys and told of marching and drilling all day, and how everyone laughed at him on the rifle range. He even dropped a handful of lead bullets trying to get faster.

When he finished, we all glanced down. Pa looked to Ma, then Andy, and asked, "Are you feeling up to telling us about how you lost your arm?"

Andy said, "Yeah, I guess I can."

He told us he was sent to a cannon team. Artillery Squad they called it. He was having so much trouble shooting the rifle, being left-handed, they thought he could do more with a big gun.

"I was the mop guy," he said, "and called on to do everything you could think of that had anything to do with water and getting it into the cannon barrel. After a cannon was fired, my job was to run the wet mop down the barrel. This was to be sure there were no hot sparks left behind. Then I dropped a pre-measured pack of gun powder in and turned the mop around and pushed it all the way down and gave it two quick thumps to be sure it was seated good. As I stepped away, another guy dropped a 12-pound ball in. When he ran back, that was the signal to fire again. Some of the guys used to yell, "Fire in the Hole", as they touched the fuse hole. When the cannon stopped banging, that was my cue to mop the barrel, reload, and fire again.

"We were drilling, trying to get better aim and get our speed up. We also were firing a new load to us, a bag of shot called 'grape-shot.' We had to be careful because when the grape-shot bag lay in the shipping box it would get deformed which made it hard to get down the barrel. We were clipping right along, started shooting 12-pound ball and, after firing about a dozen, we would drop in a bag of shot. I am not sure how we mixed up the timing, but the fuse tender touched off the cannon just as I was packing the bag pretty tight.

"I woke up at our field tent, asking who all these people were, and what they were doing here. The next time I woke up, I was on a train getting bounced all over. That is when I was told what happened and where I was going. I must have been drugged up a lot because I don't remember it hurting or even the trip, or where I was going. I just got there.

"When I awoke in a day or two, I was told what the doctor had done. He had to make my arm ready. The doctor in Boston cut off all dead and dying skin and flesh. When he got to good blood flow, he could stop. Then he trimmed the bone back enough that skin flaps would cover it and have enough padding. Then he filed the edges round so it wouldn't leave sharp edges on the bone to poke through. Next, I was turned over to his helper and a couple of nurses. Their job was to clean it all up and be sure all the crumbs from the bone saw were taken out of the wound. If anything was left behind, it would be a cause for infection and the wound might need to be reopened and cleaned out again. When they felt they had gotten it all clean, another doctor came in and stitched it up. It has not really hurt a lot, except when it got bumped."

All the time Andy was talking, I stared at his arm. The area of the wound had sloughed off some skin and drained for a while but did not look as bad as I thought it would. Of course, I had never seen an arm or leg cut off before, so I had no real idea how a good one or bad one would look. Andy's stump was dry and a good color, so I guessed it was okay. We all sat in silence as Andy spoke. I think the girls cried. I felt like it but did not.

On Monday, Ma and Andy went to our town doctor. Andy had a letter from the Army doctor who took his arm telling everything he saw and had done, and how he started caring for it and when to remove the drain that was left on the backside. The doctor took a quick look at the papers and said, "I have seen his work a lot, and you could not have gotten a better doctor if you needed your arm or leg cut off."

Ma told me later that the town doctor unwrapped the first layer of bandages and you could smell death. Our doctor would have to remove all the dead skin before he went any further. He said he'd look at his last two patients and then close for the day. He told Ma that she might want to go over to town while he and his nurse worked on Andy's arm.

She said, "If I'm going to clean it at home as often as you say it needs it, I might as well get used to it."

The doctor said, "Suit yourself but this part won't be good."

After seeing his other patients, the doctor, with Ma watching, went to work. Below the two wrapped layers that closed the cut, there were two or three layers that were stuck to the raw skin. They were very painful to pull off, and when they were off, the drain was pulled. The blood started running.

All this time, it was hard for Ma to keep Andy on the table. After a time, the doctor got my brother all fixed up and showed Ma what to do, and how to do it. He told her that if the wound got to smelling really bad, or had a bad color, to bring Andy right in, day or night. Ma was told to change the dressing every three days and if everything looked okay, to bring him back in two weeks.

At home, when Ma got ready to clean and change the dressing, she sent everyone but Pa and a live-in helper, to go outside. It was noon when she shooed everyone out and leave it to empty-headed Helen to ask, "Why do we have to leave, is he going to cry?" Ma grabbed a cast iron skillet and said, "If I hit you up-side the head with this, will you cry? Now, get out of here!"

Pa got Ma a new, small cast iron pot to boil Andy's bandages in. We were all told to never use that pot for anything else. When the water was boiling really good, she set the clock so it would boil for three full minutes. Then she added the iodine which the doctor gave her to disinfect everything with. Next, she put all the scissors and things she was using in a sock and let them lay in the water. When everything was in the water and she had it all boiling, she waited five minutes. Then it was all laid out on a cake pan to be carried to the house. Ma had already told Pa how bad it was going to hurt and how bad it would smell. It was several years before Ma and Pa even talked about how bad it was. Ma said the last time she had seen Andy cry was when he was splitting wood and slipped with the axe and chopped his foot, needing stitches. Andy cried his share when the bandages were changed and she was sure it was best to leave the wound care to her and Pa.

After we got Andy home and settled in, I got to thinking about me signing up. Andy was back and wounded and we hadn't heard from Andrew for some time. Andrew was not much of a letter writer but the one time he did write, he said there was a boy from town, Tommy Jones, who was in his outfit. Well, it worked out that, unlike my silent brother, Tommy wrote home almost every week.

So, on some Sundays after church, Ma would talk Pa into going by the Jones house to see if there was any news. Pa said Sunday was not the day to stop by someone's house if we weren't family. Anyway, they were always glad to see us and would be inviting us to stay and eat with them. Pa could see they weren't really well off and he did not want to impose on their goodwill. So, we declined the meal and just asked them for any new good news and gave them an invite to our place any time.

CHAPTER 4

I Enlist

By the Fall of 1863, the war looked like it was here to stay. Andy was getting along really well, and we had help on the farm for the cost of the food. In fact, we had so much help that Pa said he wished he had put up a bigger bunkhouse.

So, in September of 1863, I signed my name. I got on the troop train, like my brothers before me had done. What happened next worked itself out to the minute of what my brothers had said. I was sworn in, checked out, showered, shaved and in a new blue uniform in 30 minutes. When Walt, Andy and Andrew had went, they wore their best work clothes and Pa had seen to it they had good boots.

But when I was getting ready, Andy said, "Wear your worst clothes you own, and an old pair of worn-out boots. When you get there, they will give you new clothes and just burn what you're wearing, new or old. If you have good boots, you keep them. If they are worn out, they give you new ones."

He also said I would put more miles on Army boots learning how to march and do battlefield drills in one month than a couple of years home on the farm.

So, I took my brother's advice and that's what I did. Ma sewed up some pants that were about to be thrown out to the rag bag. As for boots, I wore an old pair then I greased up my good work boots and mixed up some wax to treat my leggings. If I kept my boots well greased and leggings well waxed, I could go out in any weather and stay dry. I got an old apple box and lined it with old newspaper. I put the boots inside and put the box in the back corner of our shared bedroom closet. I knew the boots would be there when I came back. I was signed on for a two-year stretch. Andy said he would keep them greased. I knew Andy would be good to his word. They would be just as I left them whether I came back in two years or four or five years. Who knew how long this war would last and what would be my part in it.

We ended up in the countryside just outside of Boston, and just like the rest said, in less than 30 minutes we were all loaded, sworn in and standing in line. We were up at 5:45 am, stood for headcount, ate breakfast, and got our gear together and were standing in the yard by 7:00 am. We were lined up in rows from tallest to shortest. They gave us Enfield rifles that had a bayonet clipped on the barrel.

Loading the Enfield took ten long steps. Miss a step and you had nothing to fight with but a ten-pound club. The bayonet was about 20 inches long with a 15-inch blade. Sometime later, the Enfield was replaced with a newer style breech loading rifles. Soldiers most liked the many models and calibers in this gun line.

We would march and drill in what was called the "yard" or sometimes the "parade grounds." All day long, it was march and drill. When we would get time on the rifle range, we were told the best range was 300 yards. But some held true aim to close to 600 yards. Someone asked why limit the range to 300 yards and was told by the range boss that we were besting rebels by 100 yards because their weapons were only good to 200 yards. This was mostly because of poor quality rebel powder and bullets. On the other hand, our rifles used a new cone-shaped Minie ball (named for some French inventor.) This was a bullet that had grooves or ridges molded in them, so they flew better and did more damage on impact. We had no way to compare the rebel rifles or ammunition, but we felt we were better off.

When we were on the range, the range boss took note that I had no trouble hitting my target at 300, 400 and 500 yards. When he asked about my shooting "luck," I told him it was a lot like hunting with my Pa's old Kentucky long rifle which was about the same weight. The biggest difference was Pa's was a flintlock and with these newer rifles we saved the new pop caps that just popped on. With Pa's old rifle, we had to prime the pan first, but not so with the pop cap.

Time passed, and it was eat, sleep, march and drill for two weeks then two days on the shooting range. On our way back to the chow hall I was told to go to the range again the next day. I thought my shooting was okay and doubted that I needed more practice, but I had learned that, in the Army, you never ask why, you just do it.

The next morning when everybody came back to the barracks from breakfast, I got my gear together and went out front. There I joined up with five other soldiers who were looking as mixed up as me. We all felt we were doing okay with shooting and couldn't understand why we were being sent to the range again. We were given a wagon ride out to the range. That was new.

Out near the range, close enough to see what was going on, there is a roof over two picnic-type tables where the brass would sometimes sit and watch. We were put out there on the firing line and told to wait for the range master to arrive. As we sat there waiting, one guy told us to look down range. We all looked and could see that somebody had set up targets way over against the hill.

A while later, someone pulled up in a wagon and one guy jumped down and talked.

"You six people have showed extra skills in the use of the general issue rifle," he said. "You all have no trouble hitting the 600-yard target."

It was sort of dawning on me what this guy was getting at.

He continued, "A new type of rifle has been taken up by the War Department and we feel you are the best to try them out."

This rifle had a lever action with a dropping breach block. Shooting it required nothing like the old loading steps. This new gun used a brass bullet casing with its primer in the base. These rifles were the first to change over to brass cases.

To start out, we were given five empty brass cases. Next, we were taught how to reload the empty cases. Everybody made the same mistake, we forgot to press in the new primer. The primers had to be pressed out from the empty shell side and into a hole in the base. The people training us were set up with everything to mold bullets, resize cases, measure powder, and they had a gauge to tell if the bullet was pressed in far enough.

One thing that no one could understand was using a polished reflector, like an eye piece. We were shown that, if we would sit back and look at the sun, a beam of light could reflect down in the bottom of the case to see if the backing for the powder was not burnt out. Eventually, we got it. So, we learned everything about reloading and caring for our new gun, but we still hadn't fired them.

Well, they finally handed out a rifle for each of us. They had a soft buckskin sling case. Also, new sling strap to put on and a shoulder bag to carry everything. A bag could carry 100 loaded brass cases. The bag also contained a stout cord to pull a cleaning patch down the barrel and a waxed pouch for the primers and a powder horn for the powder.

So now we had everything needed for our new rifle. And since we were going to be the only one shooting and caring for it, we had to give them our name and the serial number of the new rifle. After we had done all that, a wagon came with meals for us. We ate and were told that the grease from the food, and on our fingers, would smear on the barrel and breech sides. If you looked closely, you could see greasy fingerprints everywhere that was touched. We were instructed to get the small can of oil out from our equipment and wipe everything down. This was how we were to clean it every day or any time we put it away. The rifles serial number was written on the inside of the gun sleeve. We were told to get our gun and write our Army number under the gun's number. Next, we were paired up and still had never even fired them yet.

We paired up and lined up and were shown how to work the lever so we would not get our fingers pinched. We were told where and how much to oil the breech block slides and the lever action handle. If we used too much oil these parts would gather dirt.

Finally, the big time was here! We were allowed to load and fire our new rifles. We were told our new weapon would kick a bit more than the old Enfield. So, we needed to be sure the rifle butt was bedded into the meat of our shoulder and not against the collar bone or shoulder bone. We took our first shot while lying down. The gunnery sergeant told us lying down would make it less likely that we would drop our new rifle in the dirt. We were never rushed to shoot. Someone was always looking at your target with a telescope. One man in each pair shot his five shells, then his partner would shoot his.

We all reloaded and got after it again. I felt that I was doing okay but I was the last shooter to hit my 600-yard target. Although my shot landed closer to the 10 rings, I was still last. Being last at anything was not good. We spent the rest of the day reloading the protective cases we were given. Then we fired more so we each had ten brass cases, or as we now called them, bullets or shells. Our new rifles were 45-110 caliber, the biggest-ever shot.

My new rifle kicked like an old farm mule! They were first made by Christian Sharps from 1848 up to 1881 from Philadelphia. In the field, they were headed up by Hiram Bardem's new metallic cartridges which were out in the late 1860's as conversion to brass. The front sight was fixed with a split level, a Vermeer rear sight with winding adjustments. Before this sighting setup, most everybody like me just guessed at the wind. All steel parts are flat gray so not to shine and give away your hiding spot.

Eventually, we were given a two hour talk about our new rifles. We were told that we were the first to use these new rifles. Not only that, but because of the rifle's ability to shoot about twice as far as the Enfield rifles which the regular troops were using, coupled with our own marksmanship, we were now snipers. We drilled at the shooting range until we could hit a man-sized target eight out of ten times from 1,000 yards.

Chapter 5

Training for Our Target

As snipers, we had to learn to hide out and be able to shoot and not be seen from a long way off. Many of the southern outfits had been using the battle setup which the English used. The rebel troops would be lined up with every shooter backed up by another shooter. When a rebel soldier fired, a new shooter would step in front of the guy who just shot. This way as they shot, they would walk their way forward.

All the while, their general rode back and forth behind them on a horse. It may not have been the way to aim at this guy but was felt by all that shooting this one man was one way to win a battle.

Every evening as the enemy lowered his flag and fighting was done for the day, each side picked up their dead and dying. If we could kill their field general, the rebels would lose the will to fight. What I liked about this new thing was that us snipers got what to do others did not. What I liked most was being a long way from the guy I was trying to kill. I was happy to figure that out. I never was much on the idea of killing people, especially at close range.

Some of the good things that I got to enjoy as a sniper were having a new place to stay and not having to wait on everyone else to eat. It seemed to be better food too. We got new uniforms which were not bright blue and made it easier to hide. There was also a lady close by who did our washing for a month. We got more rest, better food and a better place to "live" than we had before. We never had any more marching or drilling. Instead, we spent time getting better acquainted with our "Shilo Sharps Rifle." Keeping our rifles "clean and dry oiled" was pounded into our heads every chance they got. *Dry oiled* meant everything was cleaned, then oiled and finally wiped dry with a clean, dry cloth. It was best to use a wool rag. I am not sure why, but that's what they told us. We also cleaned our re-mountable sights and placed them in the kit box that held the shells.

Then all brass casings were wiped down and we would reload any empties. One thing we would strive to do, was fire all casing so if any were bad, we could weed them out and replace them. We fired our rifles every day, shooting five or ten rounds and sometimes up to 20.

Our next step in training was how to estimate how far it was to the target. We had to load and get used to how big a standing man was at every distance. I would use the 500-yard, 750-yard and the 1, ooo-yard to set my sites on. I got used to using my thumb. I would hold my arm straight out with thumb straight up. The cuticle was the first reference point. The first mark on the right side was 500 yards. The first mark on the left side was 750 yards. The line all the way across was 1,000 yards. These lines had to be checked every month because the nail would grow out. When we stepped up to 1,200 yards, we were in a new game. It was just a far enough distance more that all the little things really made a difference. Somewhere along we were all given a single eye spotting glass. It was hard to use alone because by the time you had all things figured out and then got the rifle up, things would change.

At times, we were each shown one of four pictures of different men and told to go to the range and shoot the picture of the correct man. We were given his name but that really did not help. This is where the little spotting eye glass piece was best used. I would look for little details from the pictures, like his mustache and beard. Or he might have a crocked nose. He might have a mole or dimple on his chin. I put the eye glass on a string so I could hold it against the barrel and figure everything out. When I was ready to shoot, I could drop the glass, and the string kept it from hitting the ground. I set the sights to what I thought would be my best chance of hitting what I was aiming for.

Each time I did this, I was faced with the moment of truth. I asked myself, were all my ducks in a row? If I felt everything was good, I started to shoot. If at any time I felt something was not right, I started over. If I had any doubts, I wouldn't shoot at all. It was better not to shoot than take a shot which was not going to work. I realized that I had a lot more work to do to be able to take a shot at a live target.

We were told the rifle would shoot 1,000 yards. That was how it came from factory, and we were going to have to learn to shoot that far. The range boss asked if any of us knew how far 1,000 yards was. After a bad guess or two, he fired his sidearm pistol into the air and a guy way out there started waving a bed sheet.

"That man is Private Brown," the range boss said. "He stands 6-feet tall and is 1,000 yards from the firing line."

When assigned a practice target, we were given the general area or town he would be in, but we had to get there before he left. Next, we had to set up where the best shot would be from, and how to get there. We would wait in hiding for days while watching what our target did and when. We found that most of our targets were regular men and every morning at certain times they would go to the outhouse. We then placed ourselves where we had a double shot, and a way to hide and get away.

On the last day of training, we were set up to shoot through hog carcasses hanging up at 500 yards. This gave us a good idea of how far we could shoot and how many men it would go through. Each time I hit one, it made me remember my family and how we had worked together to butcher a hog.

On that final day, we got the big pep talk. Then we were paired up with another trained sniper. During the night, one of the pair was woken up and he left so that nobody would know which direction he went. The man who left became my shadow man. My shadow man was Chuck. We traveled separately. We each had maps of the seacoast states. Everything from the Blue Ridge Mountains, east of the water, and for the Pennsylvania state clear to Florida. We were both headed to Fredericksburg but were told to stay to the foothills of the Blue Ridge Mountains. Sometimes I walked and other times I got rides with other troops going the same way I was.

At my first drop point, I reconnected with Chuck. We stocked up on supplies and again in the middle of the night we headed out. We left as quiet as we could. Only the camp commanders knew our real identifications. We had a tent pitched on the outside row away from the other soldiers and close to the woods or other natural hiding place or cover so we could come and go without anyone knowing.

When our group broke up into two-man teams, we had been told a few things. We had predetermined targets, which were any and all rebel generals, whether in the field, on a train or any other place we saw them. Our next target was anyone wearing a southern uniform, but mostly these men were to be targeted while in battle activity. We had to do all this and be able to sneak away, so as to not get caught.

CHAPTER 6

We Head Out to Battle

We made it to Fredericksburg okay. Then we had to find the rebel camp and the top highest-ranking person there. Both these things proved to be really easy for us. We would watch them in the early morning as they got up and started moving. We found that watching the outhouses setup for the officers was the quickest way to find the officer in charge.

At our first setup, we each took two shots. We were able to center up one at the outhouse, and one at the medical tent our target was taken to after shot. Shooting the doctor who was working on that high-ranking officer was very demoralizing. On our second shot, we saw the rebels all in huddle and sending a courier to spread the word, I guess.

We were both trying to zero in on the courier and it would be just our luck that he turned and rode straight towards us. I hated to shoot a fine horse, but it had to be done. I was zeroed in on the man, and Chuck said he was set on the horse and wanted me to shoot the rebel first. As I held my breath to fine line it, I set the set trigger, a second later I bumped the second trigger, and the shot was in motion. As I looked around through my gun smoke, I saw the rider throw both his arms up and out as he fell over backwards. I had aimed for the center of the body mass. I was not a pin-point head shooter. I heard Chuck on my left saying, "Yes, yes, yes," over and over. I knew what he was talking about when I saw the horse take a nosedive and fall flat in the road. Both shots from us had hit the mark. We had forgotten for a minute that we now needed to sneak away. Luckily, we were set up in the upper room of an empty farm building. So, we dropped downstairs and headed west into the mountains.

At the start of our mission, we had dropped our main food and heavy stuff at the base of a cliff rock wall. It could be seen for miles, if you were looking for it. It was a great place to meet if we had to split up to get away.

After sneaking away from the farmhouse, we returned to the top of a tall ridge with two ridges between us and the rebel camp. We lit no fires there but just ate our jerky and watched the rebels until real late with our spy glasses. They were rearranging their tents. It looked like the officers were now set up with flat-shoe soldiers around them. They then moved their horses and mules back into the woods where we could not see them. Chuck reported that he was seeing a group that seemed to be trying to figure out where we had fired from. It took them a couple of days to find it but on the third morning, they burnt the farmhouse down. We did not see them try to track us any farther.

After a while, Chuck came up with the idea that we should go into hiding and sneak away barefoot or in our stocking feet, laying the blame on Indians. That did seem to work well. If we wore two pairs of socks, our trail looked like moccasin tracks, and it worked very well. We passed this information over to the other four snipers when we saw them.

When we met the other snipers, we learned that one of the other guys was caught the first week out. He had got too far over the line and was cornered on a long spit of land. He had followed the beach down from the Rappahannock River Bridge using the natural sand dunes to set up. He got three kills before they followed the shot trail back. He ran farther south hoping to find a boat or to be picked up by a Northern steamer moving troops and supplies south to the Fort Sumter area, but no luck. He was caught. He did not face a firing squad. They just stripped off all his stuff. When he would not tell them anything, they shot him in the back of his head and rolled him into a ditch. There were headlines and pictures in the paper for days. It took the rebels a few weeks to figure out he was a sniper and guess he was not working alone. We knew we needed more and better maps. We, for sure, did not want to end up like him.

When we returned and learned about the killed sniper, we were back in a Union field camp for a week. We needed to resupply and tend to our rifles. We did some extra cleaning and reloaded all our empties. We were surprised when our earlier request for more cases and a way to store them in the field was waiting for us when we reached the field camp. We were given fifty new cases and a metal box to keep them in. It had a tight seal over the top. So, four good meals, a good hot bath and two full nights of sleep, and we were ready to go out again. During this time, we had a good meeting with our commander, and he had maps for us. Next morning, we were gone well before first light.

Chuck had a sharp eye and would show me how he could make out the little things we needed to get our job done. When we returned to the field, one problem we had was the war and fighting had moved to flat land with few real places to hide. The only natural places we found were creeks and their cut banks.

We dropped off a couple of ridges to the west and made a nice camp by a small creek. Before dark, we got a small dry wood fire going and had a nice bed of coals for our bean pot iron skillet, and a pot for coffee. We ate beans and bacon and drank the whole pot of coffee. When finished, we put the rest of the beans, bacon and coffee grounds in the empty coffee pot. Then I kicked out the fire and wiped out the skillet with a knot of grass.

Just after dark, we packed up and headed to one of our other camps in the mountains. We traveled together but never slept together in the same camp. We split up and Chuck was going over the ridge to camp near a small pond. He joked about having fish for breakfast. I dropped down to an old farm place. There garden spot had a ¼ acre of overgrown berry bushes. If you were careful going in, so as to not leave tracks, you could crawl into the bushes and get to one of the few places where you could see out. That's where I slept, nice and peaceful. My only fear was that I might be too tired and might snore while I slept. So, I always sleep light, rifle loaded at my side and a colt revolver in my hand.

CHAPTER 7

Basswood Meets a Pine

Hid in my bushes, I woke up early to light, misty rain and a low fog. So, there was no shooting that day. Both guns checked and a quick look out before I stepped out in the early morning dew. I moved around the point of the ridge towards where Chuck was bedding down. By keeping off the trail, it was slower going, but I left no tracks. I was wearing the moccasins we had asked for at the field camp supply drop.

As I came in view of the small pond, I did not see any sign of morning smoke (which was good) but there was also no sign anywhere of Chuck's camp. The one thing that put me back in the brush was the fact that there was no bug or bird sounds. Somebody else was here, somewhere, and not too long ago. Maybe Chuck, maybe not.

As I stayed hid along the mountain side, I used my spy glass to look close at everything in the little valley. I was sweeping my glass left and right, dropping down about four feet with each pass. It was easy to see the main trail leading over the northwest rim. I could see well enough to see there were no tracks since last night's rain.

On one pass back to the right, a bird squawked and flew up out of the undergrowth. For sure, there was something over there that didn't belong. Birds on a nest don't fly up and draw attention to their nesting unless something or somebody stirs them up. Try as I might, I could see no one. The grass and weeds were too short to hide a man. Then at the last moment, a bobcat stepped into the sun, with a hatchling in his mouth. He was the reason for the bird's flash of fear.

Well, that worked itself out. Now, to keep looking for Chuck. I could see a small burn spot that might have been a campfire, but not last night. Back and forth I looked, not wanting to give up and go on without an answer. My eyes kept drawing me back to a clump of brush which looked out of place. I just could not see what was different. One thing I felt was that this kind of bush doesn't grow in clumps. There was just too many bunched together, too many plants and too tight.

Every morning and night the winds temperatures and direction would change. In the evening, the mountain air would drop down in the low spots of farmland. Now that cool air was coming back up the mountain and in a faint breeze, I got a whiff of coffee and bacon. So, Chuck was close by, I just couldn't see him. I searched for anything big enough to hide a man. The only thing I could not see into was the end of an uprooted pine tree. I just could not believe it was big enough for old Chuck to crawl into.

The next thing I smelled was someone doing their morning toilet visit, and close. For some unknown reason I looked out toward the valley. At first, I did not see anything out of whack through the thick leaves. Then, all at once I see a bare butt hanging over a log, and someone wiping it. This could not be true! I looked again at the trees.

There was a large pine tree with the top broke out where the log came from. I could not see inside. Another tree that looked like basswood and that might be a little bigger must have fallen into the pine and broke it off. I could not, for the life of me, see who it was, or guess how they got there.

As I watched, there was a splash of black water coming down like rain, but it smelled like coffee! Somebody was staying hid on purpose. This just had to be another sniper but was it Chuck?

I decided to sit back and keep watching.

A pair of tree squirrels chased each other around the broken treetops but never acted like something was amiss or a person was there. As the sun peaked fully over the east ridge, the big limbs of the basswood tree moved a little, maybe an inch. The tree was so big, the limbs stretched right above me. Whoever or whatever was making the limb move was right above me.

I only had to turn my head to see Chuck step off onto the ground. He didn't know I was there, and as he walked by me, I just stuck my foot out and tripped him. As he fell away from me, I jumped on and pushed my knuckle into his back and he froze. I could not say "hands up" without laughing a little and he knew it was me.

I said, "Chuck, what the hell were you doing up there?"

He said, "Getting a good night's sleep. How did you find me?"

I told him I never did, and that he almost crapped on my head. "Jack-ass," I said.

We had quite a laugh, and he showed me what he found up in the basswood. Someone must have put a couple boards there for a deer stand. Then the basswood fell over, striking and breaking off the pine. The pine was somewhat hollow but when it broke, four or five inches of this heavy bark wood peeled over and the two heavy limbs of the basswood on each side made a two-foot wide by close to six-foot long flat spot. The basswood was still green, so the big leaves closed off anything being seen from below.

I said, "Chuck, did I smell coffee and bacon before you almost crapped on me?"

He told me I did.

He said he got cottontails from the pond and wove a mat. Then he got as much sand from the creek as he could carry, because inside the pine trunk was just right for a small fire. He told me he has slept up there every night that we have been down in this area and just only came out the first thing before morning.

I followed Chuck's directions and walked up the trunk of the basswood, being careful not to scuff the bark and leave tracks for someone else to see. When I got up there, I could see it was as good, or better, than most of the camps we used. A full flat spot to sleep, a few broken stubs to hang stuff on and a nice place for a small, safe fire that would not be seen in the dark. This would make a nice camp to stay in, and we decided to share it. We just had to be careful that we did not leave any kind of tracks on the basswood as we climbed up. Then, because of the rain and fog, we got our gear all sorted out and hid well. Then we hoofed it back to field camp to restock.

CHAPTER 8

The Lone Sniper

We returned to the Union field camp again and walked in while everyone there was going to chow. No one said a word or even hello. It might have been because we were so dirty. We soon found out that one of the most-liked men there, the range boss, was shot while out on the range, while setting new targets. No one knows who did it and everyone was down in the dumps over it.

The lone sniper, the survivor from the two that had been sent south along the coastline the first week, was called in to oversee the range and training of troops on the range. Scuttlebutt talk was that he was not doing well. After the loss of his partner, he just could not function. He was afraid of getting caught while sneaking away after a shot. He even acted afraid of the dark. We talked with him some and told him a sure-fire way to shoot and get away.

We told him to set up on the highest vantage point and tie his horse back in the bush, a quarter mile away. Then we suggested he aim for his officer target on the other side of camp or field drills. I told him my best setup was when the rebels were doing drills or some kind of shooting. Of course, the rebels were not doing the target shooting like us, with our cannon and all, because of fear they would run out of powder.

I told him, "The next thing I would look for was the officer's tent and the closest outhouse to that tent. The rebels build an outhouse for officers, but the flat-shoe soldiers have to squat over a dig ditch. If I could get set up with an officer in the outhouse, then start shooting a little, I could shoot him on his 'throne,' and no one would know for maybe hours. If he was missed at chow time, or missed a meeting, someone might come looking for him. When found, all they had was a guy who was shot in the chest, up to four hours ago. It could be even longer. If he said he was not feeling well yesterday or last night, they could think he might have even been there overnight. They would send for the camp doctors to try and figure out how long he had been there, or how long he had been dead. With all this going on it would give you plenty of time to slowly amble away."

I don't know if our advice helped him but, in about a month he was told he could not draw snipers pay or have all the extra benefits that went along with it. If he did not get out in the field and try slowing the southern advance he would lose his sniper benefits.

He was sent to a new area always described to us as "The Rappahannock River Bridge." By closing up this bridge area, we could slow the rebel march to Fredericksburg. He had a good setup there. There were a number of good places to meet up and just let the targets come to you. In the first week, he had made contact with five targets and was able to make a hit/clean kill on each one. We met up with him and had a good pep talk with him. What it did for me was it reminded me how dangerous our jobs were. We shared with him how we did things and helped him calm his fears. He was so fearful of ending up like his first partner. We looked over his maps and showed him where he could move in the land to the west and have a good timber stand and a good-sized river.

We asked him to show us where he thought was a safe place to sleep. The very first thing about a sniper, when sleeping outside, is you better not snore. He had a small stream running off a low hill. It was anywhere from one- to three-feet wide and one- to six-inches deep where it went under a briar patch, that was 75 to 80 percent covered with thorn vines. He had crawled up the steam and put sticks across a narrow spot. He then could sleep on his little bridge without getting wet. So that was one place.

A couple of others were in farmers' barns. He said he trusted them, but we told him there was no way we would do that. We told him about our places and the drop spots where we stored our food and extra clothes. He just looked wide-eyed at us. So, we could tell he had no clue about what we were doing. We had to hope our advice helped him.

After talking with him for some time, we fixed our beans and bacon, ate what we wanted, wrapped up the rest, and pushed them down inside of our coffee pots. I could see by his face that he had no clue what we were doing.

So, I asked him, "What are you doing for breakfast or lunch tomorrow?"

I told him we were fixing it up to have three meals.

"I can brew me up a pot of coffee, fry half the bacon and half the beans, then stuff the rest in the coffeepot. That way I still had a little food left for tomorrow afternoon or evening. Then I always have a chew or two of jerky. Once I soaked some in warm coffee, but it didn't taste like jerky. So, I keep it in my coat pocket now."

We left him after dark.

We walked our way all around Fredericksburg and we made a lot of trouble for them southern boys. Chuck and I were able to hit our marks, two times each day. So, that made for four men above flat-shoes, in other words, four officers. Each of our marks had 50 to 60 men under them. It seemed they never had a second in command to take over. From what we saw when the field general went down, the rebels stopped fighting, and all carried him back to camp. A new leader was put in charge eventually but most of the time they were done for the day. This helped us a lot because there was no one looking for us. We were able to just amble away.

When the new leader took over, that officer wanted to make a good showing. He would ride back and forth behind the rows of men who were shooting and reloading. He would always try to get them to reload faster. One time we were so close to our target that Chuck heard one man say, "We can shoot faster, but who do we aim at?" There was an empty field in front of them. We knew we were too close if we could hear them talking.

After a kill, we always slipped out and went to our closest camp. We talked a little while coffee, beans and bacon were getting hot. Then we would split up and sleep. We planned to go back by their main camp and do the outhouse thing. It was so easy. The top brass wore long gray coats with white pants. They should have known their uniform gave them away from a distance. They did not realize that, with our spy glasses, we could see everything from the mountain in the west, to the central valley, where all the action started from. The valley was miles across and many miles long. There were two main roads we knew of and a lot of open farmlands where troops could camp on moment's notice.

One day, I met up with Chuck mid-morning. He said some of the officers were leaving their coats hanging on their tent pole and did their morning business at the trench with the regular troops. Chuck said they would either be facing us or have their back to us. We had planned to check out the early rebel camp. Then we would hoof it back to the Union base camp to rest, get food, and pick up traveling supplies.

That day, I was stretched out in the morning sun beside a roadside ditch, when Chuck came jogging up the road. I joined him and we jogged a bit to get miles between the rebel camp and us. When we slowed to a walk, Chuck turned up into the brush in a place where the road curved sharply west. Whenever we stopped, we could sit back with our spy glasses and see anyone coming down the road.

All the while I was with Chuck that morning, he had half a smile, half a grin. He was in a good mood over something.

Finally, I said, "Okay, what's so funny? Is the joke on me?"

"No, no," he said. "It's just that this morning, when I was setting up for my first shot, I could not keep from laughing out loud.

I said, "Well, settle down and tell me what's so funny."

So, he said, "I drew a bead on what I was sure was an officer. He was squatting across a trench with his back about a foot from the guy behind him. Then, when I shot, he kind'a stood up, but did not make it and fell to the side. And the guy he was backed up to fell over as well."

"You think you got them both with one shot?" I asked.

"It sure looked like it," Chuck said. "The second guy did not get up, and other rebels came over and they carried both men away."

Chuck and I ran the scene through our heads over and over, and every time we decided it sure looked doable. With this idea giving us added energy, we hot footed it to the Union base camp. We slipped in and was heading for a shower when a messenger boy stopped us and said the Colonel wants to see us before we go out again. So, we showered and shaved, got clean clothes and headed to the "boss tent" to see what was up, good news and bad.

When we got there, we learned that the lone sniper we'd tried so hard to wise up just could not handle things by himself. He turned in his rifle and coat patches and did not want to be a sniper anymore. Meanwhile, four other snipers got on a ship and went way south. They were trying to get close enough to Richmond to maybe get a shot at Jefferson Davis, the new southern President.

CHAPTER 9

Out With the Old,
In With the New

We were given new southern uniforms, two average horses and a set of field gear.

We headed out to get our new horses and was just about shot when we went to the horse camp to get them. Seems like no one told them we were coming. We were not wearing any uniforms at all, north or south, but had those rebel uniforms waded up in a shoulder bag. The men at the horse camp saw us in plain clothes and thought we were the south on a raid to take over their stock.

Old Chuck yelled at them, "If we were risking our asses for your horses, you would think we would take more than two."

Old Chuck raised such a fuss that a messenger, who had been up early to be on his way, was at the "trench" when he heard the loud talk. He hurried over and stepped in to save the day for us. He told the night guard he had seen us many times when we were talking really hush-hush with the camp Colonel. He was not real sure of our position, but he was certain we were not southern horse thieves.

The area guard still not believing was ready to hang us when the messenger offered to go to the main camp and get an answer. He wasted no time and jumped on the horse that had been ready for him. Over his shoulder he yelled back, "They better be alive when I return!"

In a few minutes there was a large amount of disturbance in the main camp. In the distance, we could hear horse hooves clattering on the stone in the road, and when the rider crossed the bridge there was an echo in the air. As the horse came to the gate, a lantern was held up and there sat a half-dressed, Colonel Carpenter, the camp commander. He looked a sight! He was in a knee length night shirt, pulled by the wind up to his waist which revealed he wore nothing under it. On top of his balding head was a night cap.

Well, he jumped down, but forgot he was wearing no boots, and his stockings provided no protection for his feet. He landed in rocks and mud but never showed hurt or displeasure. His first words were, "Where are they?"

We were sitting on a bench with our hands tied behind us. The guard roughly jerked us to our feet, pushed us into the light of two lanterns, and said, "Here are the southern horse thief bastards."

"Untie them," the Colonel ordered. "Get their horses and let them on their way."

Then the messenger guy rode up and stepped into the light. You could see was out of breath when he asked, "Well, sir?"

The Colonel told him he had done the right thing by coming and waking him. He also said the guards had also done the right thing by stopping us and not wanting to hang us without a trial.

Once we had our new horses, we went south and a bit west to our most southern "cache" of supplies. We dismounted and changed into our southern uniforms and stood back and looked each other over. In the past I could tell Chuck most anywhere, anytime by the clothes he wore and the way he moved. In the past, we both wore buckskin top shirts that made it easier to crawl around in the bushes. Now we both had gray jackets and pants. They weren't new and as soon as I put mine on, I saw the hole in the jacket front. These uniforms had been taken off of dead southern troops. But they were washed well because there was no blood anywhere.

Then and there, we decided we would start out with a bandana tied around our neck, but have the knot slipped to the left side. Most of the time we could see each other, and we knew where each other should be, but the bandana would help us be sure to recognize each other.

We talked many times about how we could get close enough to do our work. We decided we would have to join a group heading the right way and somehow get in the city.

CHAPTER 10

Train Hopping

Wearing our rebel uniforms, we went south and watched the troop trains come and go. We had decided to jump a train and somehow join a rebel group. We were alone in a train yard when southern troops arrived and were split up. We joined the group going north.

We rolled into South Carolina in the night. Before boarding this train, we had traveled a good way south, but went all night on a fast, nonstop train and made up the ground quick. We never were let off except when the train stopped for water or coal. Then we were let off to stretch our legs and "hit the bushes."

At one late night stop, we were given a basket of sandwiches for each car and a couple of boxes that had glass jars. These jars were about two cups big and were filled with coffee. Our car also got a basket of apples. So, we had our fill and sat cross-legged against the wall.

I watched Chuck who sat but was leaning forward. He never said anything to me, but he had ridden the "box car" before and knew if you try to sleep leaning against the wall, you run a big chance of jarring your back if this train hits a bad stretch of track. Many times, the tracks/rails of one rail company are not the same size as the others. When those two lines were linked together, you were running on a bad stretch of track. It caused the cars to jolt around a lot more.

On that ride, it pitched really hard, and I was caught in the back by a mismatched board on the inside of the car. It just smacked me, and I felt my back crack. I was not sure if I was even going to stand up. I woke up Chuck and told him what happened. He got me up and helped me stand and do my best to walk it off. As we bounced around the car, we saw others in the same shape. At least ten of us could not stand on our own.

Sometime later, when we slowed down, we were ready to offload. Chuck was going to jump down first, I would hand down our gear, and then he could help me if I needed it. Yes, I could of used more help, but it was what it was. I jumped down to a very hard, packed down roadway. There was a small lingering sting in my body, about even with the bottom of my shoulder blade. I was not great, but I was able to walk it off.

Once on the ground, we were told to head up the road. We had to go any way we could. We needed to get to a rebel camp up ahead before they stopped serving breakfast. Chuck and I had been making a lot of miles on our feet, so we got there in time. About half of the other guys did not make it. A group or two, maybe a total of 60 to 75 men, who had been on the train went almost two days without a big meal. While on this train we only got a few baskets of food and apples from the people in the little towns where we filled our water tank and coal.

As I said, some of them boys were late and they not only missed a meal, they also missed getting a tent. We were told to find an empty tent and stretch out for a few hours. If there were not enough tents, the rebels had to go to camp storehouses and see if they had anything they could use. There were two old boys who were real put out! They told us they came all the way from Western Mississippi and rode a train for two days with nothing to eat or drink.

"We have run three miles up the road to camp," they complained, "and now there's no food or even a tent to sleep in!"

The one of them said to the other, "We's a lot better off staying home."

They crawled up under a wagon bed to get a little shade. They didn't open the chow tent until evening and them two boys were first in line. When they came out, their plates were topped out with all the beans and ham they could hold, and it looked like their pockets were full as well.

When they came back by us, Chuck poked me and said, "Lokey here."

I just rolled my eyes, and Chuck knew I was thinking the same as him, which was "Here's a pair that looks out for themselves."

When evening came, a rebel sergeant came around looking for "Tom and Jerry," the two boys from Mississippi. It didn't surprise us when he never could find them for guard duty.

Next morning, we were up and ready at first light. Easy for me and Chuck since we were used to being up early and lining up for a head count. All the tents were set up everywhere, so the sergeants had to go tent to tent to roust the men. After our little group was checked, we had to pitch our tents in rows so they could keep better count of us. By noon, everything was back to normal, with all tents in rows and everybody had eaten something.

I told Chuck, "You owe me."

He asked why and I replied, "I did bet you that Tom and Jerry would be gone by morning, didn't I?"

Well, anyway, they *were* gone. The whole camp got a big speech about walking away from their duty post, going AWOL and not following orders in general.

Later that day, we were marched downtown and told they were hoping for a ship or two to be able to run the blockade of the harbor. Our job was to clear everyone out so a ship could be unloaded and not have to worry that a northern spy would sabotage it before it could get docked. They did not want to go through all this and then lose it in the harbor. Not only lose the goods, but if a ship was sunk, it would have to be salvaged so the shipping lanes in the harbor would not be blocked.

We chased all the fishermen out of the water and then moved their tables and tubs up the street to be out of the way. By the middle of the afternoon, we had all the stinky tables, tubs and barrels moved but very little fish came ashore. Then we were told to head back to camp. A ship never showed up. There were all kinds of talk about why, everything from being sunk offshore to it just never making it through the blockade.

Back at camp, we were lined up in rows in front of our tents. We were all there, except for Tom and Jerry, so they let us go to chow. After chow, we were put into small groups and given a real pep talk about our duty, the pledge we swore to when we signed up and how important our role was and how much more important it was going to get.

Our camp was set up on the outskirts of town and we had lots of visits by city dwellers, the mayor, the city council and head of the city police force. I felt the stares of these people as they watched us drill and do our other daily things. I was worried someone might point a finger at me, or at both of us, and name us as spies. And, while this might have happened to us, it never did. Tom and Jerry were gone and rumors had it they were northern spies, working their way into the ranks to get themselves close to President Jefferson Davis and the high-ranking advisers who traveled with him. These advisers were his main lifeline to everything. If a person could get close, or even be one of them, he would be in a perfect public place to carry out our job.

Chuck and me both talked about how to do it, where and when, and how close we could get. But we really wanted to be a sniper and shoot at a distance. We wanted to do the job we were trained for. By being a sniper, we stood a good chance of doing the deed and slipping away. We both had families back home and wanted to go back to them. We just needed to do our jobs and get away.

One day, after we had marched all around the City of Richmond, we came back to camp. It felt like there was a rock in my boot and I was looking forward to my bed. Chuck was ahead of me and, when he opened the tent flap, he stopped so fast that I plowed right into him. I gave him a good shove and a few choice words for stopping. Then I saw what the problem was! Our tent had been tossed, blankets off the bed, mattresses upside down and on the floor. All our stuff, personal and military, had been gone through. Someone went through our stuff to see if we were spies, or if we had any other ties to the north. We must have passed muster, because no one said who did it.

Soon, we were put into a rotation to guard a group of people. We were working our way up to a rotation which would put us with the President and his advisers. Chuck and I had not yet worked out the best way to do our job. In the four weeks we were there, Chuck marked two possible targets and I only one. We never got the chance to be out alone.

One night, Chuck hatched up a wild plan. He said every night when he took a trip to the "trench" he would walk by "Tiny's" tent, and the man would be there snoring away. Chuck had seen him lay his rifle between the sleeping pad and the side of the tent. Now Old Chuck thinks he can sneak out and use Tiny's rifle. That way if Chuck had to, he could use, then ditch, Tiny's rifle and head back to our tent. If anyone came looking, we were "sleeping," and our rifles would be clean and cold.

CHAPTER 11

Time to Strike

Old Chuck decided to try his plan. He slipped out about midnight and did it without a hitch. He had no problem getting Tiny's rifle and belt pouch. A quick trip to the "trench" and off into the dark he went. I lay there in the dark, wide awake, just waiting and listening for a shot or something that would tell me Chuck was working.

Then, way off in the dark I heard a lone gun shot, then a lot of horses running, and then people shouting. I figured we would be called to formation, so I got my boots on. I was careful, not putting on my socks and buttoning up my shirt crooked. I did not want anyone to know I had been awake. All the while I knew Chuck was out there. My thoughts and nerves were on edge, wondering if they shot and killed him. Then they would come and question me. If Chuck was caught alive, they may torture him and find us and me out before I could run. I kinda made up my mind that we needed to get out of this behind the lines stuff. We were not getting any closer to doing our job. Four weeks and we were no nearer than we'd been in the first week

There was a lot of shouting and men running by when the back tent flap slipped open. Chuck slid in without a sound. It was so quiet I could hear Chuck breathing and his heart pounding. Next, as I thought it would happen, we were rolled out. We were made to stand in front of our tent and wait for the sergeant in charge of night watch. He sent a detail of three to check if everything was as it should be in the middle of the night, in a tent compound. Also, as I thought, our guns were checked to see if any fresh mud or grass were stuck to them. They even checked the knees of our pants!

Not sure what else they would of checked if they'd taken time. But we had just got the "what was wrong" story from them when there was a lot of yelling and cussing coming from the tent rows forward, and three tents over. As the detail took off on the run, we were ordered to stay in our tent until morning chow call.

Our tent was small. It was just big enough for two men and the few things we had. That included a small backpack, a rain slicker, two blankets and a couple of shoulder bags and a powder horn. The only thing we carried, but never used, was the kit to make our own bullets. Like everyone else, we got all we needed in the way of bullets and powder from the camp supply.

This supply set up was a cross between an Army storehouse and a general store. The only other thing they had was an office, or really just a desk, for the paymaster. We would all line up on payday, get our Confederate coins and paper, then most guys would head right to the counter of the general store. Most of the guys would spend all their pay before leaving the store. The biggest seller was the small bottles of whiskey. You got about four big swallows from it, enough to wet your whistle, but not get drunk. The store also had the assortment of pens and paper which you would need if you were writing any mail home. The only good thing I saw in this whole set up was if you were sending a letter home, the camp commander would buy the stamp.

Well, I finally got a chance to talk to Chuck. As I was saying, we had a small two-man tent. We were lucky, though, because whoever was there before us had two short legged sleeping cots. It was better than sleeping on the cold ground, but less leg room. We sat facing each other, and I had my right leg between his two. Now I could lean into Chuck and talk quietly without being overheard. To add to this, one of us would put our jackets over our heads, making the odds even better that we could safely talk.

Chuck said, "I went around camp to where the officers were put up in nice walled tents. Most of them slept two men and they had a make-shift wardrobe dividing them off. The highest in rank had a two-part tent, with the sleeping area in the back, and a small cot behind a drop cloth for their personal aide. In the front tent they had a small picnic-type table with two benches and one large chair set at the far end. There was a small fold-up writing desk with a fold-up stool for the aide to take notes and make reports."

Chuck said he always felt he could line up two or maybe even three offi-cers for one shot. It's just that these men were too drunk to sit at the table in a row. So, since he couldn't get more than one officer in a single shot, there was no reason to give away his hand.

After seeing his first plan was not going to work out, Chuck had to come up with another target to make this all worth it. As he was returning, he came past the horse holding pen. As one part of the pen got really mud-dy, the rebels would move the horses a little farther out and put more hay down. As Chuck came along the north side of the pen, he could see instead of a regular fence they just had a rope pulled tight between two trees and a rock. The rope let the rebels increase the size of the pen without rebuild-ing the main sides or walking in the knee-deep mud. After some looking, Chuck found a guy on the ground, one guy asleep and a group of four close to drunk. As he worked a plan in his head, he found that getting a sight bead on someone in the dark was not going to be enough for all he went through to get where he was.

He explained, "My first move was to loosen the rope on the far side by untying the knot and cutting it. Then I used a sharp stick pushed through the rope ends to keep it up and together until it was pushed on. Then I went to the far end and got into the new hay pile. The horses all saw me and followed me to the lower roped end. Now I cut the next stretch of rope and then did the same thing by sticking a stick through it. One more quick trip to the haystack had all the horses and mules crowding against the rope. When it went down, they all rushed forward and found out they were free.

New hay did not hold a candle to knee-deep green grass. The drunk party of guards were really slow to see the stock leaving. One guy was put out for sure, but the others were just about asleep. Someone making a visit to the trench sounded the alarm. I ran into the horse camp before anyone could respond. I shot one rebel point blank from about four feet and was sure it went through one guy and into another. I was high stepping it out of there before anyone came running or could I.D. me. I had to head around below the trench and slip the rifle under the tent flap before anybody was awake enough to understand what was happening."

We sat there in the dark listening, and so glad we took the extra steps to cover our trail. Chuck had brought his moccasins along and was wearing them during his night's outing. We had a ground cloth in our tent and had turned it up so we could cut a piece of sod out of the grass we were standing in. This was for just the kind'a thing we needed to do tonight, where we had to hide something quick, and now his moccasins were under that flap of sod.

After our talk, we went out and put our jackets on the ground and sat cross-legged in front of our tent. We were enjoying the sights as a small division of mounted troops ran by. They were sure they were on the heels of horse thieves. As they went out of ear shot, we could hear the goings-on up front in the camp. The fresh-fired rifle had been found, and they were sure they had their man. So, as they took Tiny to the lock-up to face and be questioned by the camp colonel, we decided it was not worth anything trying to get next to their president this way. So, we packed up and took our leave under the cover of the night.

We were about ten miles from where we left our cache, so we had to hot foot it cross country so as not to leave footprints on the road. Now cross country was okay, but we did have to ford a river and a couple of creeks. The river was much easier to cross than the little streams. The river had bridges, and the decking boards left no tracks. But the little streams were tough. They only had dirt or mud banks so we had to find a narrow spot or a tree lying across which we could use. We made it to our cache with just enough time to gather our stuff and slip back into the thick pine cover. We hid our southern army stuff and headed back to our own base camp.

As we got close to the base camp, we could sense something was wrong. We did not hear or smell anything what should have told us that camp was on the other side of the hill. And, as we topped the hill, we could see why. Camp was gone! Oh, you could tell it was once there but now gone.

CHAPTER 12

The Train Depot

We were not too worried about finding our fellow soldiers. We took a quick pass around the southern side of the deserted camp and found no trail. We came in from the west and saw nothing, so it was east or north. So, north, it was. Their tracks coming from the field all went north. We could see where they turned out of the country and off to the northwest and now were on a hard main road. This road led right into a small town, and a railroad depot. We had to find someone who could tell us if they got on a train, and if so, where did they go?

A little wandering around told us more of what we were now sure of. Just outside of town we found where a tent city had been set up. You could see where everyone had walked going and coming from chow hall. There were two very worn trails that led away from the center of camp and over a small hill. We stood on the hill and were able to see where everybody went. The trail to the left was to a small meadow that had a nice creek flowing through it. The one to the right was the trail to the "trench."

All forces of any size had to have a trench. When you had a group of 300 to 400 camped for more than two days, a trench was dug, and rules were in place so every man could deal with their own waste. That meant you used the trench and covered your business before you left.

There was always a detail of misfits who were assigned to different jobs around the camp. The best would be washing dishes. The worst was "working the trenches." When you worked the trench, you followed the string line set out by someone who had decided how far apart, how wide, and how deep. You just did not want the waste laying on top of the ground, and you did not want the trench too wide or too deep. You had to make sure you were not overloading the ground from the standpoint of too much waste would find its way into the water supply.

Anyway, by the time we got there everybody had come and gone. We were sure they boarded a train here, but to where, we did not know. So, we worked out a plan to find out. We were down to about two days' worth of jerky, and only a little cash between us. We might pay for one train ticket, or some food at the general store, and no train ticket for either of us. So, we started to the train station. Chuck asked how long it had been since they pulled out and where were they going. The train master told us about two to three weeks, and they did not go all at once. Seems they were waiting for something. Two riders were sent out each morning going south and returning in the mid-afternoon. We told him we were scouting south and lost our horses, then we missed the camp moving to the north.

"I thought they were looking and waiting for someone," the train master said. "I guess it was you two."

We didn't know how much to trust this man. So, we played along with him. We told him we needed to catch up to them. He told us they were headed to Harper's Ferry, West Virginia. He told us when we were ready to travel, he would get us on a train going that way. We told him we did not have ticket money, and he said the Railroad had a deal with the northern government to move people and staff, so he would get the money back.

He also surprised us when he asked about us eating. We told him we were down to moldy jerky, and he took one look at our jerky and pitched it to an old dog sitting in the shade. He told us to follow him. We went to the general store, and he talked to the owner.

"These two boys were guarding the rear of the troops moving up here and they lost their horses and could not get here in time to catch the train," he said. He went on to say, "Their friends spent a lot of money with you, I would guess about a year's worth any other time, so you should be able to outfit these young men."

The store owner responded, "Be glad to."

We got a small skillet, coffee pot, two tin cups, two slabs of side meat (bacon), four cans of beans, four cans of pork, about ten large potatoes, two onions and about a dozen apples and eggs. The only extra we could ask for was a small sack of hard candy. He looked up, as if to say something, and Chuck said we got dried out in the sun and they helped.

Next morning, when we headed back to the depot, we had more stash than we ever had, but we did not know where we were going, so we took it all. By the time we reached the depot, the agent told us we missed our train that morning.

"It will return tomorrow," he said. "But going the wrong way."

So, we had a full day and a half to rest up and wait. He also told us we could camp in the grove behind his barn, and if a big storm blew in, we could slip into the back of his barn. So, we were set with everything but a tent. We were used to a lot less, so we would be okay.

I woke up to the smell of coffee and bacon frying. It smelled so good. When I rolled over, Chuck was sitting on a rock with a cup of coffee and a bacon sandwich. Seeing him, I was awake, and my head cleared.

I asked, "Chuck, you baked that bread?"

He said, "No, the storekeeper had his wife bake it and bring it over last night. I met him by the barn while doing a walk around of our camp. This camp is working out really well. I drank my coffee and the egg and bacon sandwich. I started thinking what happened to our coffee pot and skillet. We both had one at one time."

I had no answer about the missing coffee pots and skillets. All I knew was we had left them behind in the camp that was pulled up when the rest moved out.

Several hours later, we got our train and bid the station master goodbye. We headed northwest, jumping around between Virginia, West Virginia and Maryland. We rode for two days, just traveling. We were at a station somewhere and told all the seats were full of paying passengers and we would need to move to an empty boxcar, or the mail car at the end. We chose the mail car, reminding us of our ride into Richmond. We were assured it would stop where we wanted to get off. So, we crawled into a corner and napped until a big jolt got our attention. This is your stop, the postal worker told us.

We jumped down and had to walk along the track bed to get to the station. It was crossing a small muddy creek that we both shied away from. There was no room to walk beside train cars, so we had to wait for people and luggage to be unloaded and more people to get on. Then, with a loud chug, the train started to move. We started walking up the tracks for a good two city blocks before we came to the depot platform.

Chapter 13

Colonel Adams

We hung around the depot platform for a while until we felt we were being watched. Then we slipped over to hide under the cover of a pine tree and a big bush, but we could see who came or went on the train, or along the street into town. Less than an hour went by when Chuck spied a wagon going past, being pulled by four good sized mules. We held back jumping out in the road until we were sure the driver was wearing a blue uniform. Then Chuck jumped out and hailed the driver while I kept a bead on him from the shadows.

Chuck asked, "Where's the main campground?"

The driver was a little surprised but settled right down when he saw Chuck's blue uniform. The driver replied, "Going there as soon as I make another stop, so climb on."

We went down the main street until he stopped at the general store. Then two men came outside with their arms loaded with cured hams, sides of bacon and two rear quarters of beef. They threw them in the back, so we settled up front. One of the guys came up towards the front and gave the driver a paper that was no doubt a bill. We went on down the street and turned into an empty lot, then pulled in behind a big building. The door rolled open, and we got two bags of flour thrown in on top of us. Chuck asked if this was the last stop and was assured it was.

"We will be back to camp by dark," the driver told Chuck. It turned out, he was right.

Once we hit the camp, it was not hard finding the Colonel's tent with all the flags flapping, and a nice row of double tents pitched on high ground, under shade from the afternoon sun. I was close enough to ask, and I only had to ask once where Colonel Carpenter's tent was, and we were told to sit at a table under a rainfly.

By and by, a couple of men walked up, and I could see he had the arm bars of a colonel, so we stood up. Old Chuck, just being a little nervous, started to tell him our story before this officer even asked.

"Where is Colonel Carpenter?" I asked.

Then we were told Colonel Carpenter had been moved back to somewhere close to Washington, D.C.

This new colonel said, "I have taken his place and I'm Colonel Adams." He told us he had been briefed by Colonel Carpenter about us and what we were doing. As for our coming and going in the dark, as long as we checked with him, we could carry on.

So, Chuck thanked Colonel Adams and asked about our tent and things we left in the old camp. We were handed off to another guy who must have been a second or even third down the ladder.

He just said, "Follow me," and took off at a brisk walk.

We followed and stopped at a big tent where supplies were kept. A regular flat shoe took us in the back and pointed to a big box that looked like a casket to me. He said he was put in charge of gathering our stuff and packing it away. He had a paper with everything listed on it. First thing we checked was our Sharps rifles and everything that went with them. Everything seemed to be in order, so Chuck checked off his paper and we lugged it out. We were dragging the box out front and realized we had no tent or ground cloth. So, back in we went, and Chuck got us a nice two-wall tent and a big ground cloth. The flat shoe carried an armload of stakes and odd ropes that were needed to pitch it. He yelled at a guy who brought up a small wagon, pulled by one mule. We piled all our gear in and climbed on. The flat shoe gave the driver orders, and we were off. He said he knew we would want an outside row, close to the woods, or a big bush row. The spot we were taken to was just right, outside by the trees.

We decided to use the driver to help with the box and pitching the tent and, with his help, we finished up our afternoon in the chow line. Chuck told the cook to come to our tent before lockdown and bring a medium sized box. The cook showed up right on time and we unloaded our packs into the box. We gave the cook tomatoes, eggs, onions, and all but the four apples we had left. We had the liquid from the apples and jerky while we were on the train. He said he had no use for the jerky. We offered him our small skillets and coffee pots, but he said he had no use for them either. So, we kept them and the coffee. That night, we had a good sleep

The next morning, we got in chow line early and left word that we wanted to speak with Colonel Adams. His orderly, a houseboy, flagged us down and told us that Colonel Adams would see us at 11:00 a.m. So, we took a stroll down to the holding pen for the horses. We sat in the shade and talked to the hosteler about horses. We told him about Chuck's nighttime visit to a rebel horse pen and what he had seen and done. Chuck told him where guards were sitting and where they should be. We left him scratching his head and rode to our meeting with Colonel Adams.

We were a little early, but that worked out really well. The Colonel was just finishing up with some small brass people and was ready for us. As always, Chuck did most of the talking. He told the Colonel how we had been clear south to Richmond in hopes of getting a shot on their southern president, and how hard it was to get on a detail that would get us close to him. We got a chuckle out of him when Chuck told him about the horse pen and how we lost our horses along with the rest but could change ours to the better now we were in a northern camp.

The next day we were allowed to take two horses and get a feel for the area. We worked our way back and forth from the mountains to the west to the broad valley in the east. We were sure we were going to have to travel a good way south before finding any southern troops to ambush. We found a great spot to leave the horses on an old mountain farm that was rundown and let go. I was headed to the berry patch in the garden for a place to sleep. As I worked on hands and knees, I bumped my knee on something hard that moved a little. A few pokes with my finger found the edge of a board that was nailed to other boards. When I was able to lift it up a little, I saw it was a cover for a spring house.

I went exploring and found this was dug down about five feet and about six feet square. There were shelves made of flat stones sitting in the water. There were about a dozen clay crocks sitting on shelves just above water level, so they would not be in the water but be low enough down that they did not freeze. I found the stick used to hold the door up and found that the first step was high enough that sleeping on it would not be damp. So, it was good enough for me.

The next morning, I met Chuck at the horses and had a little time to look the old barn over. It was small but tidy and clean. We could close the horses inside and sleep if the weather got cold or wet. We peeked in the windows of the house and found it to be not much. It looked like the last people there gathered up the kitchen and clothes and left. We had no plans of going in or staying there, but we wanted to know if anyone else was coming or going. To do this, we got a wind-broken tree limb from the woods and laid it in the path, a little against the door. It would be very easy to see if someone had pushed past and went in. Then we took a small smear of mud, like mud doper wasps would use, and pushed it in the slide track of each window. So, if someone opened the window, it would fall out and we would be aware of their presence.

We were now in sniper mode, on our own and making a plan. We could see through our spotting scopes when the southern army front had been setting up an ambush spot. We did not see the reason but drew some pictures and made notes. There was a stretch of road that ran about three miles where it was mostly through cut banks and ran below the ditches and fields. We could see where any group going south on the road could be attacked by rebels hidden on the sides and in the fields. We were able to see where they had dug in cannons. It looked to us like they planned to mow down as many troops as they could, once they started firing. We even spotted a shooter's nest in a big oak tree, about midway up the road, and 100 yards to the side. They were planning to have a sniper there or someone to work as a forward spotter. We both put that in the book so when the time came, we would have a record of where it was.

We drifted south along the mountain front, looking for anything that would tell us where the rebels had been. We got as far south as our first cache and sleeping camp was. We checked out the area for any changes and found none. We had two horses that were trained to stay out on a picket pin, tied to a leg. They never gave us any trouble and would be okay until we came back. We built a small fire and brewed a pot of coffee. We had a few slices of thick bacon and split our only can of beans. I started a second pot of coffee to have a jump on the morning.

We knew we had to get the information on the road, the cannon and the possible ambush site back to our camp and Colonel Adams. Chuck said he would keep watch and nose around some while I rode back to report in. I was not much of a horse rider. Back home, we always hitched a buggy. I got my pack evened up and as light as I could, reloaded the Sharps and made sure the powder looked dry. Chuck thought it was best to get fresh powder, though, because it had been in the box for about two months. We did not know if it had been in any rain. That was okay with me, for sure dry powder was best.

I left out before first light. I did not want to be spotted on the road too close to our cache and night camps. I got a good four or five miles in and was making a good clip up the road. I really didn't see anyone except people on two or three farms in and around the barn lots. Only one person waved but all saw me pass. As I neared the countryside around Harper's Ferry, West Virginia, it was no longer river bottoms and farms, but small mountain farms that raised a lot of sheep and kept a milk cow or goat for milk. I knew there were woodsmen in these parts too. Men who would hunt and trap and get along with a different way of life.

As I rode along, the road narrowed down to just wide enough trails which followed the valleys and ridges until you got to where you wanted to be. Unfortunately, I picked the wrong trail/road and thought I could just walk over the ridge and get where I wanted to be. Well, wrong move. The way was steep, and I had to lead my horse to make the top, but could now see where I was, and where I wanted to be. I had to backtrack about three miles and would get there in time for noon chow call, but it was not so easy going. As I got closer, I could see everything I thought I would see around a tent city camp. I made my horse walk a couple of miles to dry off the sweat, then took him to the creek for a good drink.

Eventually, I rode up to a so-so gate, a pole and a counterbalance and a young flat shoe puffed up his chest and said, "Who goes there? What's your business?"

That was a new first for me. I told him I was reporting to Colonel Adams.

He only had to have someone take me to him. Instead, he kept asking about what my business was. I just told him it was classified, and I could not say anything else to him about it.

He now had a bead on me and told me to dismount. When I did, another guy who I did not see stepped up behind me and put one big hand on my shoulder and the other on my Sharps.

"Wait a minute," the guy said, "You are one of them sniper-spy guys. I remember you at the first basic camp." He went on to say, "They took six or eight of you off the range and we never heard what happened until Colonel Carpenter told us where he moved you."

This man who recognized me told the young gate guard to get someone to care for my horse. Then he walked with me up the hill to where I knew I would find Colonel Adams.

We sat at an empty table under a tarp for shade. Colonel Adams was talking with five or six men who were field generals from the looks of them. When he saw me, he called a halt to the meeting and waved me over.

"Something special must be happening for you to be here in the middle of the day," he said.

"Yes," I told him. "I think so."

Then, instead of reporting, I started asking several questions. "First," I asked, "are these officers field generals? Do they have troops in the field?"

They all nodded yes, and I started to tell them what Chuck and I had seen.

While I talked, Colonel Adams waved his aide over and sent him on an errand. The aide came back with a map of the area I was talking about. This map had something I had never seen before. There were lines that told you where the mountains were and about how high they were. These lines showed the flat farmland and the mountains to the west, where we had our sleeping camps and our caches.

Using these maps, we were able to locate the stretch of road where I had seen the rebels building bunkers. I pointed out where I thought the forward spotter was at. This report put everyone in a good mood. They had indeed planned to travel down that road in order to flank the southern troops who were making a push towards the east.

At some point, Colonel Adams waved to his aide and a rainfly was put up around us. This puzzled me because I never saw anything that looked like rain, so I stood with hat in hand, waiting for them to finish.

Under the cover of the rainfly, Colonel Adams pulled us all in close and said, "We have an informer in our midst. Only six, or maybe seven, knew we were planning to march down that road. We wanted to flank them with a force of three divisions, or 600 men. It would include about 100 horses and four artillery battalions. Then a whole bunch of support people to follow."

Colonel Adams said we were very fortunate to have me arrive and report to them before the northern force broke camp and headed out. Now the Colonel would have to make other plans, including a counterattack. At this time, his aide and two flat shoes brought several trays of food. Our noon meal was delivered to our table, from cold water in real glasses, to coffee in heavy porcelain mugs.

After the meal, Colonel Adams asked me if I could find my way back in the dark, enough to lead some hand-picked soldiers back, and how long it would take. I told him if we left at 8:00 p.m. it would take 25 to 30 minutes to get over the mountain. Then three to four hours to get far enough south that we could leave the road and go cross country so no one would see us or our tracks on the road. We should be able to get into the timber ridges of the mountains before dawn. So, he told me to return to my tent and rest until someone came for me.

I said, "Yes, sir. But I need to stop at the supply tent first."

It was about 6:00 p.m. when a soft hand shook my shoulder. As always, I came up with my revolver first. The young peach fuzz trooper was aware of this and pushed the muzzle away with a smooth swat of one arm, as he stepped out of reach of a knife from my other.

"I was told to tread easy," he said. "I heard I had to watch for my revolver and my knife."

I packed my stuff, and we headed to the main tent. As we walked along, the trooper said, "You're in good standing with the Colonel. He thinks the work you are doing is great. When you snipers started your work, the south slowed down and since then they have made little headway."

Colonel Adams had a big meal set out for us. I sat at the end of a broad table, across from Colonel Adams. Four field generals filled the other four chairs. We were served and the Colonel's aide closed the rainfly. Between bites, he filled me in and gave me the last-minute details from the rest. Colonel Adams said one word and his aide slipped through the corner curtain.

I asked, "It's private walls here?"

Without a word, the aide slipped out and I could hear him walking around and saying something to someone. By the shadows on the rainfly, I could see there were guards posted at each corner. After talking to the guards, the aide poked his head in and nodded to Colonel Adams, then he slipped out again.

Colonel Adams said we were going to have to keep our voices down.

"Someone may be hearing more than he should," he said.

He pushed his dishes away and rolled the new map out. I grabbed the empty tray and piled the dishes on, then slipped down to his end of the table. Some one had made marks on the map in chalk so, if needed, those markings could be wiped away in a flash.

CHAPTER 14

A Girl Named Sue

As we studied the new map, I could see that the four cannon encampments Chuck and I had spotted were marked and all the bulwarks chalked in. The new plan was to disable the cannon and set gunpowder charges at the base of all wooden bulwarks. The hard part of the plan was to move men down south, behind close hills, and set up our own cannon sites.

The officers pitched back and forth with ideas about how many men it would take and where to start. So that was the plan. The only thing I was interested in was the six men who had been picked to go with me that night. They would sabotage the rebel works.

Later on, it was coming up on twilight when a group of riders came up and they were leading a MULE! I asked why that was, and it seemed these horses and some mules were caught running loose on a road, so they were put in our holding lot. As they were used, it was found they were all southern animals and all well-gaited. This meant they were natural trotters with smooth and comfortable gaits, the mule included.

So, I got my first mule ride. We headed out and I briefly told the rest where I wanted to go. They turned off the road and dropped into a creek bed where we allowed them to drink. My mule only took a couple of big slugs and stepped out of the creek. The horses just about had to be dragged away. We kept to the woods for a few miles then came out on the back side of a farm field. From there we hit the road. We weren't used to gaiting horses, so I did not realize how fast we were going, and how far we had gone. One of the soldiers rode up beside me and told me the horses needed to slow down a little. We slowed to a walk and went to the nearest creek for water. The horse riders got off so they could keep control of their horse's heads. Only two or three quick swallows and that was enough for them. My mule put her head down and only acted like she was just smelling it. Then she took two quick sips and turned away.

Back on the road we go, and my mule starts slowing down and looking ahead real hard. When we did stop, she would not stand quiet. Instead, she kept looking up the road. I petted her neck and tried to calm her. Then one of the guys said, "I hear horses coming." So, we jumped the ditch and stood in the bushes of a fenced row.

In a couple of minutes, I could hear them myself. Four riders went by on the road, and we let them go up the road some.

One guy said, "Good thing you heard them."

I replied, "Not me, this mule heard them first."

We led our horses back on the road and the other guy said the rest needed to dismount and walk a little to get the kinks out. I walked with them but realized I was in good shape, not stiffened up or tired at all. As I walked, the mule followed behind and matched my speed, and when I stopped, she stopped too, never coming close to running into me. That was one good thing over my last horse. If we were walking and stopped, he'd keep going and step on my feet. I could see I had a much better mount than those other riders. She was not dripping wet, or winded, or showed any signs of being tired. If I turned, she would follow without dragging on the reins. I had never had any experiences with mules, but if they were all like this, I would use them all the time.

We went another eight to ten minutes on foot. I was on the road. I stopped and mounted up. Then I told the others to ride at a walk and not talk until we got past the two farms up against the mountain's east slope. We were all past them when the farm dog started barking, and shortly after, a gruff voice called out, "Shut up you damn dog!"

Just another 100 yards and we were around to the point of the mountain. My only fear was how to keep this troop of seven on horses from being seen. Best stop for the day. So, I took them to set up a camp. We found a tight, leafy thicket and stepped down and let the cinch on our saddle off to let the animals breathe easy. I asked if anyone had a rain slicker, and they all said yes. So, I got two of those slickers stretched between two trees and built a small fire. That coffee and bacon was well taken. We ate and drank and talked in hushed voices.

After eating, I told the men to tie their horses well and drop their saddles. Leaving the animals, we walked up the mountain to the point so that we could see over to the stretch of road they wanted to get to. They took turns looking through their spy glass. I got my glass and told them I was leaving.

When going back down the slope, we got to the horses sooner than going up. Knowing they had their own plan for in the morning, I bid them farewell, slipped off into the trees, and went west into the mountains where Chuck and I had left our first cache. I checked on it and took the jerky and left some fresh in its place. I went to the closest cooking camp and found dirt covering hot coals. Chuck had been there recent. So, I made a cross in the ash, a sign for Chuck, and went to my sleeping camp. It was in a real thick brushy spot, surrounded by briars. There was an old dead tree in the middle, and I could lay on the big slab of bark to sleep and be up off the damp ground.

Once there, I tied my mule well and set the gear aside. I took a look around and did not see anything out of order. When the night birds and bugs started to talk, I knew I was okay. If they stopped, I would know something was wrong and to watch out.

I woke in the next morning and, as I had trained myself at the post, I just laid there listening with my pistol in my hand. I was hearing the daytime birds and bugs which told me everything was okay. I cocked my head around and did not see my mule.

"Shit", I said and sat up.

She was gone. As I sat there, I thought how could someone slip in here and get her without me hearing? I mean she was less than ten feet from my feet. I sat up and this move was greeted with a solid push to the middle of the back. A chill went through me, and I let my revolver drop into my lap and slowly lifted my hands. I expected to get the back of my head smashed in by a gun butt or a ball at any time.

I said, "Just be easy, okay? We might be on the same side."

When no one spoke, I slowly turned around and let out a long breath, that I did not know I was holding. There, laying up against the same old log was my mule. Why was she loose? Was somebody was pulling this trick on me?

"Chuck, are you there?" I asked out loud. Nothing, silence.

How did she get untied and walk past me without stepping on me? Then to turn around and lay down no noise?

Well, it seemed like she had done all that on her own and silent. I was going to keep this to myself, no one would believe me. I petted her nose and talked softly to her and then started to roll my bed up. When I looked back, she was up on her feet without a sound. There seemed to be only one answer. I figured it out; I must have gone deaf!

I saddled up and ambled down the mountain. By the way the mule's ears were acting, I could tell something was up ahead and I knew it long before I smelled Chuck's coffee. She was sure that something out of the norm was happening up ahead. Ah, yes, there was Chuck!

"Well," he says, "look who's back and riding a donkey. You get a demotion or something to lower you to riding that long-eared thing?"

I told him no, that it was just what they had. I wasn't ready to tell him about last night or this morning.

We talked some and Chuck said he was able to get across the valley and hit a couple of targets, one each day. He had to get where other shooting was going on so they couldn't pin down his shot. I told him what our soldiers were planning for the road, and how they think someone told the south of their plans to march along a body of troops down far enough to flank the south's main body. It was a plan which they hoped would stop or at least shorten the war.

Chuck and I decided to get up to our favorite lookout and see what we could see of our men. We spotted two of them right off, working around one of the cannons that had to be hidden under a bush. I could not make out what they were doing.

Just then, Chuck says, "Those guys by the cannon are wedging the barrel."

That made sense to me. If the cannon is loaded it's really easy to just push a wedge in beside the ball so when it's fired, the ball can't come out. Most of the time it wrecks the cannon. Maybe it can explode to the point of killing those around it.

If it's not loaded, you would make a mix of mud and mortar and push it down the barrel, trying to almost fill the barrel. When the mix dries, there's no way to get a ball down it. One must chip and chisel until all of it is cleared out. Most of the wedged barrels I heard about were just sent back to the foundry to be melted down and remolded into a new cannon.

While we watched, we could see that the rest of the guys were digging in order to plant charges into the bases of the bulwarks. They planned to blow them up, but I did not know how they would light a fuse or set a charge off.

Then Chuck came up with a great idea. He said we could shoot the charges and set them off from behind the mountain. However, that did not go over with me since I figured the bullet would be cool by the time it got there.

We were not able to puzzle out how our men could set off the charge. But we figured they know what they are doing. So, we went across the valley and started to look for a new camping spot. We were never happy over there since we felt safer in the old spots that we had used before. We worked close together and left a little earlier to get to some active war shooting. We already knew how much shooting the enemy leader would d0 to the enemy's plans.

One day we went too far and started to ride down a little town street. Right off Chuck half yells "Retreat!"

I asked no questions, or why. I guessed we had been spotted or that Chuck had seen somebody we could target. I just wheeled around and returned back the same way we came, ducking off at the first place the horses could go. Doing this, we got away from even the fastest shooter. We planned to head for any high ground and see about shooting back into town. My mule jumped the ditch and scooted behind an old shed. I jumped down and saw what had spooked Chuck. Several riders were coming our way.

At that time, I lost track of Chuck but there was no time to look for him. I drew a bead on the first rider. When the dust cleared, that man was headfirst on the ground. I just jammed another shell into my Sharps and got ready. By the time I was ready to shoot again, they were way too close. I'm used to shooting at 500 yards or more, where it isn't as personal.

The lead rider had twisted his body around to yell something to those following, two uniformed men. Then he spotted me, and his horse was running full out and had its head kinda low.

"This is it," I said, and pulled the second trigger. When the dust cleared, the front two men fell off their horses and were rolling in the road. So, Chuck was right, "Line them up and shoot two at a time!" Well, with three of them down, the rest lost their will to chase us. I reloaded just in case they did, knowing if that happened, I would have to run for it because they would be on top of me.

I was lucky. The last two riders just loaded their dead friends and headed back up the road. Then it dawned on me, they were still in range, and they wouldn't chase now. So, I wiped my eyes and pulled the second trigger again. Then there was only one left. The ability of the Sharps rifle always showed itself. At close range it would easily go through two men. If three were lined up proper, you might even kill the first two and have a third man in sad shape.

One thing we were told more than once, if you kill someone, they're done, but if you wound someone, it will take him and another one to take him out of the fight. I was more a long-range shooter because from 500 yards it was no longer personal. You could see no focus before or after a shot. Lots of times we never stayed put, just drifted back away so as not to be found. We had a good ten minutes to move and still use our spotting scopes to see any changes done.

As I mentioned earlier, the best has always been to shoot the field general. When he was hit or killed., the men just gathered everything up and retreated back to their camp, to fight another day. In the heat of a battle, one never knew where the shots were coming from.

One time, I did shoot four men with three shots, but I did not plan to do anything like that. At that minute, I was in a shoot-or-be-shot situation and had to shoot at close range. Then again, I took that shot as the targets were going away. I grew up in a close family. We had no big secrets or held grudges. We worked things out. I didn't mind being close then. Here it was shoot or run, I never wanted to face anyone before I shot at him. It was not personal, just my thing.

I stood real still and listened for shots from the south. I heard nothing and guessed Chuck was on the run or maybe in trouble or even dead. Those last two things would be bad. Chuck and I had talked between us about the south getting our rifles. We sure did not want that to happen and right then and there I decided I was going to start carrying more shells, ready to fire. Right then the ten rounds I had been carrying seemed a bit too few.

But today I was sure the riders had given up and I was, for now, out of danger. I went back and gathered all my empties, wiped them clean and put them in my bag. Then, I went to look for my mule. I had to hide behind the shed and didn't have time to get her neck rope down and tie her. I had jumped off and dropped both reins.

When I came around the shed, there she stood. From her tracks, the only moving she had done was stomping flies. She was right where I had stepped off. She looked and acted like she was glad to see me. She pointed her ears towards me and lowered her head. As I got close, she rubbed her nose on my arm, so I petted her a little and talked in whispers to her. As I went to get on her, as always, she stood still and never moved until I said "go" or bumped her with my heels. I took note that she was always ready, and spurs were not needed. I just had to do a little smack, a kiss sound and we were off to the western mountains to try and find Chuck.

As I traveled the road in twilight, I felt safe. As I rode my mule, I experimented with how to make her go from one gait to another. It was mostly just a little touch with my hands, and she would step up the pace. At the very top, she just rolled into a smooth canter, and then to an all-out gallop. So, it was interesting to me. I had never ridden a horse trained as well and as willing as this mule. With me moving one toe, she would side-pass over and back. My riding horse at home also had to pull the buggy, single and double and I imagined my mule would be up to it.

The last thing I found was her reaction to stray horses and people smells. She would perk up her ears and stare right to where they were hiding, or where they had been. As we came up the road, I could see a rider silhouetted against the sky as he topped the hills ahead. Him and me were riding in the same direction and I wanted to catch him up. I asked the mule for a little more speed, and we just went a little faster.

She seemed to know we were after the man up ahead and moved over to the edge of the road so her feet did not make so much noise on the hard surface. As we got closer, I knew I would be cutting off to the west soon. I thought my turn off should be just anywhere now. I squinted into the dark to find it. When I looked up, the rider was gone. I had no idea who he was, or where he had gone.

I had got started calling my mule, Sue. It was a fitting name that I could say and not be too bad. All of a sudden, I saw my trail and headed Sue up the fence line. She was all stiff and alert for some reason and she was not as willing as usual. When we trotted up over the first hill, Sue stopped, stood crossways in the trail and blew a hard whistling snort. Her ears were trained forward, and she was staring at a good-sized bush. Then I realized she was pointing out someone, or something in the cover along the trail. With the smallest amount of pressure on her bit, she backed up, nice and slow and quiet. I remember other times that she had acted this way, and it would end up being someone hiding on a road or trail. So, Sue was sure there was someone hiding up ahead. Where did that rider on the road back there go?

CHAPTER 15

The Lone Rider

I had lost sight of the rider up ahead and I was getting nervous. I did not want to shoot the Sharps at close range and in the dark. I was not good with the reloader. I needed to reveal who it was. I slipped the reins over Sue's head to be sure she would be there when I got back. Then, in a rather chicken shit move, I slid off her on the right side, to keep her between me and the unknown. I waited for all the night bugs to start again before I moved. Then I pulled my pistol and got down on hands and knees to get below any wild shooting in the dark.

As I inched forward, I heard Sue again, but not as loud. It was more of a low kick. I was hoping she would not give me away. A few feet further, brought me to the trail of a rider. He was still mounted and facing away, like he rode in and just stopped. The only thing I could do was cross the trail and get close enough to see who it was, or what he was doing. While I creeped along on hands and knees, the 'skeeters were eating me up. Just then, the unknown rider's horse stopped and shook his head hard. I guess they were bothering him as well.

In the shadows it was easy to cross the road. I could see him looking back into the darkness that hid Sue. I was really close, and his horse's head was twisting from side to side to keep an eye on me. I was surprised the rider did not catch on. With the horse moving like that, you would think he would catch on that somebody or something was coming up behind him. As I got within three feet, I saw the barrel of a Sharps rifle hanging on the right side. It was then that I realized it must be Chuck.

But, instead of saying anything, I moved along his right side and set myself up for a foolish move. I moved the revolver to my left hand and brought it up next to his right ear. As I cocked it next to his ear, I put my left hand over his pistol as he was trying to draw it. It was so quiet; you could hear a heartbeat. Chuck just froze. As he slowly turned his head, I put the muzzle next to his right cheek. I stopped him turning anymore and we all stood quiet for a time.

At last, Chuck said, "Shoot me or something; I got to get these pesky 'skeeters off me."

The bugs must have been terrible because he didn't wait for a reply. He slapped at the pests, and while he was at it, I withdrew a little so he could not see me in the dark. He whirled around his old horse and there was no one there!

"Okay," he said, "you got this drop on me. Step out of the brush."

When I did, he had the most surprised look on his face I had ever seen.

"Why the hell?" he asked. "Where did you come from? Where is your horse?"

I let out a small chuckle and headed up the back trail to find Sue. As I hoped, she was right where I left her. She was covered with bugs but only swished her tail. I rubbed my coat over her face, and she rubbed me back. Something no horse has ever done. She only moved her head and tail until I was getting ready to mount. Then she just faced out a front leg and I stepped up.

After that, me and Chuck rode in total quiet until we got to a cache and eating camp. I checked on the cache and took a circle around to see if our trail blocks had been moved. We would pull a grass runner across the trail. If anyone came through it would be gone. All was well, though.

As we settled in, Chuck wanted to know the whole story, from when we split up to when we met on the trail. I told him about getting caught behind a shed and having to shoot fast. I told him I aimed and shot at the first rider, but two fell.

"They stopped in their tracks and gave me time to reload the big Sharps," I said. "Then, as they caught up to the riderless horses and stopped to see to their dead friends, I picked off one more. Then I reloaded while they tied that guy up. The big Sharps was resting on a fence post that was set against the building, so they could not see much movement. As they went back down the road, I could see they were in the range I am used to shooting. So, I pulled the second trigger, when the dust settled, there was only one left.

"I drifted deeper in the bush, listening for anyone hunting my trail, or any shots from the direction you took. As the sun went down, I drifted back to the edge of town and nothing was in an uproar, as if you had been caught. So, I rode the ditch in the road until I got on the main road north. Still no sight of you so we just drifted north to cut off trail. Somewhere down the road I could see you ahead. The mule told me you were in the bush along the trail."

"Well," he asked, "how come I did not hear or see you on the road?"

I told him I stayed on the shaded side and rode on the soft shoulder to not make much noise.

"Old Sue horse," I explained, "was interested in you back on the road. She had drawn a bead on you or your horse like a scent hound and she walked right up to your hiding hole."

I told Chuck she was the first mule I ever rode or had been around. I told him what I liked best about her so far was how alert she was. When I got off and dropped the reins, with a pat on the neck, she would stand right there, not so much as shuffle her feet until I returned. After I had puffed her up with praise, we laid a plan for the next day.

CHAPTER 16

Teaching the Children

Early next day, Chuck and me were on the road. We wanted to know more about the little town we ran from yesterday. We wanted to know if a big group was nearby. We stepped right up along the road, retracing our steps.

After the first four or five minutes, Chuck asked, "Tell me again where did you get that gaited mule?"

I told him about when I ran for camp last week, he was the only ride rested up. The four guys who came back with me had picked her out for me and had her all tacked up. I didn't know anything about this mule, or mules in general, as far as that goes. I did not tell Chuck anything about her special talents, so that he would not ask to trade. I just realized how much I liked Old Sue and did not want to give her up.

As we rode along, I noticed that, first thing in the morning, his horse had wet spots starting to show around his flanks. When we stopped and stepped off, Sue just blew through her nose like she was getting rid of a pesky bug. Then she quietly stood in the shade and didn't make any more noises and stood still. But Chuck's horse blew through his nose several times and stomped all four of his feet. A quick check over showed nothing significant.

We hit the road, stopped now and then, and used our spy glasses to search the ditch banks and fields for any army activity. Then we moved forward to the next high spot, searched everywhere, and moved on. I found the ditch and fence row where I came onto the road while getting away from the southern calvary that we figured was chasing us.

Later, we rode right past the shed I had been shooting from. After a better look, I could see I got off lucky. If I would not have knocked the first two riders off their horses, they might have headed right up to the shed and had me surrounded, and most likely shot me. The fact that I killed four riders with three shots, put a little fear into the rebels and gave us respect.

Of course we did not wear northern uniforms, so us being northern snipers was not known to them. Yesterday's shots were so close that most any mountain man worth his salt could have made the same shots with a good squirrel rifle.

As Chuck and I rode on we met and talked to farmers who asked us where we were from. We always told them western Ohio, 30 minutes from the Kentucky and Tennessee line. We said we were drifters looking for work until we decided which side to join.

We took care to hide our Sharps, long barreled rifles, so I stuck a fishing pole down alongside the rifle and left just the end showing. I would tell anyone who took notice that while drifting and having to rustle up our own grub, we went past a lot of ponds and creeks that were fishable. We needed to eat more of that jerky and fish now and then was a nice change.

We said we would trade work for food and any news about the war. Many times, people tried to get us into talk of the war, but we told them we were from the west and had no experience with slaves.

While we were being careful, I kept my opinions to myself. But I could see why southern plantation owners would want and need slaves. I hadn't heard of a landowner having over 1,000 acres, though. With the southern men away at war, one mom with two gown boys, working three times a day, could not take care of all things that needed to be done, and on time. On the other hand, I also could see that a man being worked seven days a week for no pay would want to be free.

Anyhow, Chuck and me could talk a good story and of course we would never tell anyone we were northern snipers and say that our job was to disrupt the southern army all that we could.

On account of my fishing story, we got the okay to fish in a guy's pond and the stream that went through his farm. We caught four or five keepers apiece. We gutted them and packed them in cool green grass. Then we hot footed it to the top of the first ridge line to the east. When we got our spy glasses into use, we could see what we were looking for. At the most southern that we could see, there was large tent city. Then, ten miles from that, there was a small 40 tent camp and a small lot with horses. About ten more miles north of there was an active skirmish line. I could just faintly hear the small guns, but I could see that the close valley was filling up with gun powder smoke.

We knew we needed to get to the tent camp and battle front. Every field general we put out of service would be a day his company does not shoot. When we downed a high rank officer, his men seemed to be giving him a king's departure. The rebels circled around the body to protect it, and a two-man stretcher team was brought in and the wounded or dead general would be carried to a small four-wheel wagon. Then they would make four lines behind the wagon and walk back to camp.

In camp, he was looked over by what was a camp doctor. After that, he would be taken to a tent setup in the back, in some heavy shaded trees, waiting for a trip to a train. With any luck, he was sent in a pine box.

The next day we said our goodbyes to the farmer who had let us fish and headed out with a sack of jerky, our four smoked fish and a big chunk of bacon. Chuck said we had enough coffee, so back to the real world. We cut across the farmer's wood lot for two reasons: it would get us on the main road east and not have to go through the town. We always had our eyes open for safe camping sites. We found a faster running stream and several fresh thickets so we could make that spot work. We worked our way past farms. Some had people on them and some didn't. We did not want any dogs barking at us, so it made cutting new country tough.

It was easy enough to find the fighting. Then we slipped back and camped in the woods. It was always new experience sleeping in a new place for the first couple of nights. It was completely dark when we got to the stream. We ate smoked fish with no fire.

After supper, for some reason, Sue would not settle down. I stood up on a dead fall and saw the reason Sue was upset. Way off in the trees was the flicker of a small campfire. I jumped down and covered our heads so Chuck and me could talk about it and decide what to do without being heard. We decided to get closer and see who it was. I went one way and Chuck went the other, both agreeing not to shoot until we had to. As I got closer, I could smell wood smoke. Now on hands and knees, I could hear hushed talking but could not tell what they were saying.

I got as close as I dared, and saw they were a group of black people. There were four men, five ladies and a few kids. I couldn't see any weapons, so I felt safe when I got the nerve to talk.

When I said, "Hello the camp!" they jumped ten feet high!

My surprise had their eyes as big as saucers. They could not believe how I got so close to them. I knew they were hiding and did not raise my voice. I told them they were safe with us. We weren't there to take them back.

As I talked and said, "We" and "Us," I saw these people were puzzled and I could tell they did not know that Chuck was ten feet behind them. So, when Chuck spoke, one poor old lady fell to her knees in surprise.

They were not cooking anything, so we told them to put the fire out, and then we showed them how to hang a blanket and a couple of shirts to hide the flame. Then to cover it well so no one could see it passing by. They had run away about two weeks ago but were having trouble moving around unseen with so many people. We told them they might find less people over to the west against the mountains. Their biggest problem was going to be food. They had cleaned out the plantation smokehouse before they left. They had been setting food aside for two months before a break to run showed itself.

The biggest thing they had, and I had never seen before, was putting fresh eggs in lime water. They got the lime to pickle up hams and pork shoulders, mixed the powder and water up and carried them in a water skin. If they didn't break, they could last five or six months.

They had everything they needed except a couple of guns. Now, in these times, it was easy getting a gun, unless you were black. So, I set them up with a plan. Take all the men and any boys big enough to be in the army. I told them to sneak in close to where the soldiers would be fighting tomorrow and do anything they saw needing done, or anything someone tells them to do. Easiest way is to help the shot-up men back to the doctor's tent in their camp. If they were lucky enough, he might die on the trip.

If the wounded man died, I told them to take everything, bullets, shot, powder and primers. I told them most everything should be around their necks on a strap. I reminded them not to forget to get a good rifle with a bayonet. To also look for belt knives, staying away from anything that had a name, or initials carved or anything painted different.

I also told them to keep their eyes open for any kind of pocket or money belts. The money would buy them train tickets. I added to be careful that no one sees them "rob the bodies." I told them they should sign up to work as a wagon boss. Then when things were right, they could head out. I drew them a crude map and pointed them north. We said our goodbyes and retreated for the night. If they hold behind it there, they would have a better chance.

CHAPTER 17

The Next Game Plan

Next morning, we got up early but didn't see any of the blacks. We kept watching as rebels took load after load back to their camp. We found a target and easy. There were skirmish lines as far as we could see. One thing we did see was a faster push to go north. Our picking off two or three generals a day no longer had the effect as it did at first.

This meant it was time to check back in with our field camp. We had one piece of news we were sure Colonel Adams would want to hear. One of the black men said that, while looking for food, they came across a train sitting on a siding and pushed way down the tracks away from a town. Any car that was not in the trees was covered with green tops and fresh cut tree limbs with lots of leaves. The train was loaded with army stuff owned by the southern army! So, it was decided they were moving north by train, but just how far, we had to find out.

We were on the road before first light and only took from our cache, gun powder and primer caps for our new shells. We were traveling north when we ran across more people going north than any other time. We were careful passing groups of men, not sure if they were farmers going with their families, or southern troops doing what we were doing. If they were, they sure weren't outfitted for it.

We had no trouble cutting west through the mountains. I found a well-used trail and went north-west until signs of a settlement started to show.

We found the field camp easy and we also found our tent and personal stuff right where I left it. We unloaded our food at the cook's shack. He was always surprised when we brought food back. To repay us, he would have fresh coffee and a fresh pie or cake on the table in the storage room.

We went to care for our mounts, now that they were cooled down and relaxed. We told the hostler to give them special care because we would need them first thing in the morning. He sent his helper for the blacksmith. We told him again not to let anyone else take them. In fact, we told him that, if he had another mule like this one, we would trade the horse.

Hearing this, he said, "You're happy with the mule?"

I just nodded my head.

He smiled and said, "These were the best trained mules, or horses I have ever seen." He poked Chuck in the gut and asked, "You want to trade"?

Chuck just shook his head.

The hostler said, "These are the first rides I ever saw that would lay down on command to let you on, then get up when you were ready."

I asked why that was important and he explained that if we were shot in the leg and could not get up and on, the animal would lay down for you. Also, if we were caught in bushy country, we could both lay down to hide. I am not sure I would do that. Most likely I would try to run, then to hide with some trees or a rock cover.

Our message to Colonel Adams had us at his table for early supper. We told him what we were dealing with and the trainload of stuff the black people told us about.

"That news really changes plans," he said. "You two could use a hot bath and a shave, then sleep until I call you."

We followed his advice but before I got my turn in the hot bath, I took a walk past the holding pen. I did not see my mule or Chuck's horse anywhere. A knot dropped in my stomach. I jumped right to the worst result, believing someone had taken them to use.

I did not do any training on my mule, but Chuck had worked his horse a good bit. One thing Chuck taught his horse was to come to a low whistle.

He was also good about not blowing through his nose to call to a strange horse going by.

As for Sue, she was all trained up and I took it for granted. She was trained from someone else's hard work and I was really liking my mule and did not want to lose her. In fact, I had the hostler on the lookout for a mule for Chuck. The hostler was sure they had got two mules when they gathered them up running down the road. They could quite possibly have the animals from the night camp Chuck had raided.

Anyhow, I was worried. I found the camp sergeant and asked about our mule and horse. He was none too friendly. He was spouting out about me not having a personal hold on any one animal unless I was to personally own it.

I was getting nowhere but all sudden-like, when he was done spouting, the sergeant said, "Seen him leading two mules towards the blacksmith set-up."

I headed that way. The blacksmith setup was a good-sized tent and two 10 x 10 rain flaps. The place was set up behind a thicket, and below a little hill. There were four "smitty's" there, working around the clock. All hours of the day and night something would come in broken, and it was their job to fix them up again.

When I got there, one man was asleep snoring up a storm. Another one had just finished fixing a broken axle on a wagon and was putting the wheel back on. The third was shoeing my mule! Tied to the rail beside her was another mule, a dead ringer for her. The only difference, he was a gelding.

I looked this new mule over really good and as far as I could tell he was great! One of the smitty's said he had taken both out to town when they first came in. They were for sure a pair. They had to have come from the same farm, and both trained by somebody who knew their business. They were by far the best mules the smitty had ever seen and might even be better than the everyday riding horses.

I told him to be sure they were not checked out for use by anyone else, even for a day. We needed the mules for their toughness and their trained handling. He said he would bring them to our tent when he was done. He said there was a little clearing in the brush behind our tent, and they would get fed and tied up there with plenty of hay.

"They will be in the dark shadows," he said, "real cool and not be seen, I PROMISE!"

After hearing all this, I rushed back to our tent. Chuck was snoring away when I got there. At first, I did not recognize him, and thought I was in the wrong tent. I saw a few pieces of clothing that were in a small trunk wardrobe that were mine, so I laid down. When I laid down, I jumped right up again. I had forgotten that my Sharps was covered up in the bed. I moved it and settled back down. I was happy that everything had gotten right, and I fell asleep.

When I woke up, Chuck was sitting on his bunk cleaning his Sharps.

I asked, "Is it morning, or night, or what? We were to meet with Colonel Adams, and we must have slept right past our meeting."

"No," Chuck said, "when I woke there was a note pinned to a tent pole in the doorway that said, 'When you two wake, come to Colonel Adams' tent.' Below that part, the note added, 'We took your mules to water and feed and gave them a good rub down. Then we put them in the back with plenty of hay.'

I jumped up and looked for my boots to go check.

"Stay put," Chuck told me. "They are there all right."

I put on my boots anyway and we headed to Colonel Adams' tent. His aide met us at the table and told us he would get us our dinner and have Colonel Adams join us. He had the kitchen workers each carrying a tray and he had the coffee pot and a stack of cups. He told us to eat, and he would call the Colonel when we were about done.

As we ate, the aide brought in three field generals and two flat shoes. The generals sat down to coffee and pie. The flat shoes put up the rain flaps again. Just as our dishes were cleared away, Colonel Adams slipped in. We all stood and were given the short wave that meant "at ease."

We got introduced around and told how important our work was.

"These are the two who reported the loaded train," the Colonel said. "We have a few prisoners in the lock up and one is a shopkeeper and easy to lean on. He told us everything we needed to know. The south was making a big push north and wanted to get all the way to the Maryland-Pennsylvania border by spring. To move like that would give the rebels a big jump ahead and give them the chance to move west and the north to outflank us somewhere in Central Pennsylvania. We think they are trying to get to a new arsenal at or closer to Shippensburg."

We were told that we would move north somewhere in under a week. Colonel Adams had scouts out to get the lay of the land and find the best places to be. Colonel Adams dismissed the other three but held us for more talk. First thing he said was a man's name and his aide stepped in. He told him to lay out the maps that were on his bunk. When he was back, Colonel Adams took them and told him, "Walk along with these men to their tent and bring their Sharps rifles back and all the gear.

As we walked to our tent, we asked the aide what was up, but he didn't say anything. So, we walked in silence down and back. When we got back, our old shooting instructor, the range boss, was sitting there with a few papers in front of him. He asked to see our Sharps and asked if we would unload them first. He checked the serial number against our names and asked if we still had a complete reloading kit. He was happy the guns were the ones checked out in our names two years ago, and the kit and their boxes were in good shape, clean and well-oiled. The last thing he checked was if our spare bullet casings were in good shape and clean.

He was very happy and handed both Sharps over to another man that we hadn't noticed before. This man was from the company that made our rifles, and he checked several things. The set triggers were checked first, then the lever that worked the breach block. Then, using some type of gauge plug, he checked the chambers. Then he looked over the detachable rear sights. He wiped it down and handed the rifles back to Chuck and me. He told us that both rifles looked well cared for and were holding up well. With that, he stood up and nodded his head and said, "Colonel Adams", and walked away.

Colonel Adams told us the problem. He explained that they were never able to talk with the two men who went to the Fort Sumter area almost two years ago.

"The one man who got killed," the Colonel explained, "we know about that. And we know his partner could not work alone. Meantime, you two are having no trouble. At one time, we overran a small to medium sized rebel camp and in their storeroom was one of our Sharps, the one which was sent out with the man who was killed. The rebels were not using it because they did not have any brass casing or the tools to reload it. We did not find full or empty shells or any leather shoulder bags."

Colonel Adams did not think there would be any way we could find the missing things if we went south. Richmond had been farmed for all it was worth, and the war was now moved a couple hundred miles north. He said the rebels were trying to get a win at a place called Wildness Battlefield, a few miles to the west of Fredericksburg, Virginia. Win or lose it looked like the rebels planned to move north on a train.

CHAPTER 18

Pie and Coffee

Following the meeting with Colonel Adams, we were sent to the first mountain west of Frederick, Maryland, to stop a flanking move. We set up camp to the south of Frederick. As we usually do, we set up on the west side, up against the timber. We always came and went in the dark and liked nobody knowing when we moved around. We slipped out the first night to get a feel for things in the valley to the south and east of Frederick. We could see little dots of light in the farmhouses and a few places where there were clusters of houses.

Later, in the daylight, sitting up on the slope of the mountain, we could pick out church steeples. One afternoon, Chuck spotted a group coming up the valley. There was enough trees and twigs to hide who they were. When they stopped, Chuck said he would sneak up and see what he could find. I was to get back to the base camp and make sure Colonel Adams knew what we seen. Chuck said he would take a closer look and would be back as soon as he could.

I left for base camp right away. When I rode in, Sue was a little hot, so I had to tend to her. I was lucky enough to find a hostler who knew me and that man took over the care of Sue. He and I went to my tent where I stripped off all her gear and left it in my tent. Then I gave Sue over to the hostler's care and went looking for Colonel Adams. As I cut across the camp, I found his aide. He said Colonel Adams was at his tent eating. He said I should go to the tent, and he would see to it someone brought me a tray with coffee and real cloth napkins. I told him I did not feel right sitting at the Colonel's table without him asking.

"No, no don't worry," the aide said. "The Colonel speaks very highly of you and Mr. Chuck. In fact, he would be mad at me for not sending you."

I went to the Colonel's tent and found he was not there, so I just sat down. The Colonel knew I was there when he came in carrying his plate tray and coffee cup. His aide had a pot of coffee and fresh pie.

When the Colonel came in, I stood up and said, "Sir."

He said, "At ease."

I remained standing and he looked at me.

Then I asked, "May I speak frankly?"

"Yes," he replied. "By all means, yes."

I turned to his aide and said, "If you get the curtains, I'll help you hang them."

He told me there was no need and that I needed to sit down and eat, and that he would do it.

I turned to Colonel Adams and asked if there were any field generals in camp. Before he could reply, his aide spoke up and said there was some on the way.

"With your permission, sir," I told the Colonel, "I'll wait to say my piece until the generals come."

"As you wish," said the Colonel.

By the time we were down to pie and coffee, everyone was there and seated. I asked the aide if there were people posted outside in the dark. He never replied, just stepped back out. As he did, I started to talk, but the Colonel tapped his fork against his coffee cup and when I looked at him, he put his finger against his lips, signaling me to wait. After a few short minutes, the curtain waved, and the aide stuck his head in.

"Colonel Adams," the aide said. And when the Colonel looked at him, he just nodded his head, and the Colonel nodded back.

Colonel Adams half stood, then nodded in my direction, and asked me to talk.

"Sir," I said, "I hope you don't think I'm blowing smoke just to get a good meal, but when Chuck and I were on patrol, we saw a long column of dust coming in the valley along the base of the mountain. It looked to be a couple of miles or longer and moving south. I was sure it was a long column of troops who were following the road."

At this point, the Colonel's aide came in with maps rolled up in his arms.

"Good," said the Colonel and everyone started looking for the map that included the Town of Frederick and the countryside south of that town. Our first point was for me to show them where our camp was. Then we looked for the roads heading south. It took a while, but I was able to find where we were when we spotted the dust cloud.

Everybody came around the table and crowded in close as the Colonel sat beside me. I stood up and tried to move away, but he said, "Stay put, we need you to tell us everything you know."

So, I sat back down, and the Colonel continued, "Everyone at ease. Speak your mind and ask questions, just do it quietly."

I started to point out where I was and where I saw the dust. Just then there was a ruckus outside.

I heard the Colonel yell out, "James!" which I took to be the name of his aide.

As he responded back, another loud voice was yelling in and saying he needed to see Colonel Adams.

I jumped up and said, "That's Chuck's voice." And about then the rain flap opened, and the red-faced aide was being backed through the gap, right up to the table. Guns were coming out, and one of the guards from outside came in and put a revolver to Chuck's head.

"Colonel," the guard said. "Do you want me to shoot him?"

"No!" I yelled. "That's Chuck! He is with me!"

"Good work," the Colonel told the guard. "But stand down now and go back to your post."

When order was restored, I said to Chuck, "Man, you're going to get out of this war real fast coming in like that."

Chuck excused himself to the Colonel and said he had more news to tell.

The first words the Colonel said were, "You eat." When Chuck told him no, the Colonel yelled in a high voice, "James!"

His aide came in with two others carrying a large plate tray with beef and beans and coffee for Chuck. The Colonel told them thanks, and they nodded and left.

Between mouth bites, Chuck pointed out more to whoever wanted to know more.

"I went up the road and came to a little grove of trees. Sudden, like so many drones, men ran out and surrounded me real fast. They asked all kinds of questions and asked if I was thinking about stealing their herd. There was a dozen or so men and they had about 100 heads of beef, and some nice lookers. The rest must have been raised in the brush because they were kind'a skinny. I told them there was an open field about two miles up the road with a big creek on the far side, be a good place to camp for the night and close to town. From there, I told them, they could head out first light and be to the rail head depot by mid-morning or noon. They said they wanted to sell their herd before any renegades took them. When they asked what I intended, I told them, 'You see me riding south don't you? And you see I'm alone and I can't be a problem for you.' Well, they let me go, then I rode on south, until I was sure they weren't following me. Then I cut back and, as I went by, I counted 10 to 12 riders, two old supply wagons and a couple of other men that kept out of sight in the trees."

One of the field generals asked how he could tell there were other men if they were out of sight.

"Bob's never wrong," Chuck replied as he finished his pie and coffee.

It was up to me to explain who Bob was.

"Bob is Chuck's mule," I explained. "Mine is named Sue. Both our mules have ways of letting us know if someone is close by and trying to hide."

Most times, after reporting, we would be gone at sunup the next day. This was the first time we held over to help with plans to take charge of the development. They brought out the new maps, the ones with elevation lines which told us how high places were. The plan was to capture the cattle. It was worked out to line the fields on both sides of the road with mounted and flat shoe divisions.

Those troops were to stay out of sight unless the men and cattle made a run for it. We still were not sure where the herd was going, but the northern army could use fresh beef. We would try to buy them. If they were honest farmers, driving their herd to market, they should be willing to sell to us. But if they had already made a deal with the southern army, they would not be so ready to give them to us. Having troops hidden and ready meant we could take the cattle as needed.

CHAPTER 19

The Paymaster and the Doctor

Using the new maps, we could see where the men and their cattle were camping and how we would sneak in and get around. We took up our positions in the dark. When they headed out in the morning, we had a detail of ten mounted soldiers meet them on the road. We asked who they were, and where they were going, and what they were going to do when they got there.

They claimed they were selling their cattle on the eastern market and Frederick was the main, east-bound span for livestock. They wanted to sell before someone came in and stole them during the night. They did not want to lose any more family in a shoot out to save the cattle and horses.

At this point we just shook our heads and agreed. We told them the Colonel back in camp might be interested because we needed the beef as well. We told them to keep going up the road at a slow walk and we could count what they had as they went by. They had a herd of cattle pushed by 15 riders. They had a remainder of about 50 horses and mules. They had three wagons for supplies and chuck wagon, and these were pulled by a total of 12 mules. They agreed to our plan, so we picked a ditch bank which they would pass, and two on each side counted cows, two counted horses and two counted mules.

When the count was done, they had 333 cows, 45 horses and 20 mules, they needed to keep the extra horses and mules to pull wagons and get back home. We left them in a field a mile south of the railyard and told them to stay put until the Colonel and the paymaster could talk. If their men wanted to go to town, we would post a guard with the herd. This would help us and them.

The next morning, around 10:00 am, Colonel Adams sent word to the in-charge cow man that he should come to our camp. We were going to buy every animal that had a trail brand on it. We did not want to buy any animal they might have stolen along the way.

When the head cow man came to see about the sale, he didn't come alone. There was a group of a half-dozen with him. Chuck and I just happened to be at the Colonel's tent. His aide had asked us to stand by in case the drifters were really southerners and showed up in force. Because the whole thing was uncertain, I told James the aide that he might want to talk Colonel Adams into staying in his tent while the paymaster and him handled this deal.

As for the cows, I never saw a big buff on the hoof before, but I was told the chief cook and one of his helpers took a detachment to look them over. If they felt they had enough flesh on them, they would drive three or four back to camp to be butchered tonight. If the butchering went well and the meat was okay, that would be a signal to paymaster to pay them.

So, the paymaster had got the okay and it was time to do the deal. It was getting late in the day and fires were lit. The paymaster asked who was the owner, or the spokesman for the cattle sale. A tall man stepped forward. I can still see him and remember his name. He was from a place which he called Bugtussell, Virginia. He called himself Amir McIntosh. He was one of those people you don't forget. Like I said, he was over six feet tall and not fat, even though he looked like he weighed some 300 pounds. He wore a worn-out buckskin coat over a wooly shirt. He was wearing a bought pair of black wool pants that were patched in both knees and the seat. When he spoke, you could see one tooth missing, but the one next to it was gold.

Being in the gun business, so to say, I used my gun as a tool to do my job. This being said, I always took note of the guns that others were carrying and how they used and took care of them. When I looked at McIntosh's weapons, I saw newer model revolvers, clean and well worn. Overall, his handgun riggings were well-built and well-beveled. As he walked, the revolvers stayed within fingers' reach. The holster, swinging back and forth, was never tipping to pitch the guns out or under the edge of his coat. The handles were of a dark wood and the guns were a dark blue, probably put on by the factory to ward off rust. The high lines on the guns were worn and shining from being put in and out of the holsters.

The front row of the men standing beside McIntosh were as set up as he was. They whispered among themselves and rocked back and forth on their boot heels. They formed a circle around us. Chuck made eye contact with me across the circle, and he twitched his head to tell me to back out and meet him around behind the group.

"Something's not right," Chuck whispered. "There are too many of them and they're too well armed to just be collecting the money for the sale of a small herd of cattle."

Chuck pointed out that, along their belts were knives at everyone's waist, but each one had another knife on their backs between their shoulder blades that they were trying to hide. I motioned to James to come over and one look brought him over.

"We have them on all sides," James whispered. "So, when the shooting starts, hit the ground."

Me and Chuck felt better knowing that we weren't the only one thinking about the danger they could cause being so close and so well armed. Chuck and I drifted to a spot behind a small trash wagon which was sitting outside the cook's tent. As we watched, the drones started to drift around. They were moving really close to the paymaster.

For a time, they haggled back and forth until they came to an agreement. I felt the worst was over. But Chuck told me to stay awake while the paymaster made out a bill of sale and was having Mr. McIntosh sign it. The paymaster's helper had opened the gold chest and was counting out the money. It was easy to see there was a lot more in the box than was needed to close today's sale.

Seeing the gold, all the drones took a step closer, and all said, "OH! HA!" and pointed at the gold.

"Stand back please," said one of the paymaster guards.

Well, no one did, and in fact they all moved forward.

Then, out of nowhere, Chuck fired his Sharps at one man and yelled, "Stay put!"

The man was hit in the hand. Everyone froze in their tracks.

Mr. McIntosh questioned Chuck, "What in the hell are you shooting my man for?"

Chuck came forward, reloading as he walked, and said, "This man had pulled his belt knife and was headed for the paymaster."

Mr. McIntosh said, "We'll see." He started walking towards the man but was stopped.

"We'll get a doctor for him," Chuck said as he stood up on a wood box. He continued, "You drones show your weapons. All of them! Your pistols, your rifles, your knives, everything. Now come out here in the fire light and sit down or be shot down." Nobody moved, so Chuck cocked the lever on his rifle once, and they all complied.

Moments later, several northern troops came out of the dark, the drones really gave up. They put their weapons on the ground and backed away.

There were 13 of them. We did not body-search them, but we gathered up 13 loaded rifles, 16 revolvers and 21 long blade belt knives. The guns were all loaded, and the knives were razor sharp.

We got a short bench for the guy with the shot hand. Lanterns were brought close. Many times, the guy said, "You didn't have to shoot me."

Chuck would always reply back, "How far did you think you were going to get with your pig sticker out and flanking up our paymaster?"

When the doctor got there, the man shut up. The money was counted out twice and Mr. McIntosh put it in his saddle bags. He told all of his men to go back to where they tied their horses and stay together. He said he would be there shortly.

The doctor said, "This man needs to stay here in my camp overnight. You know he'll be safe, so come back early afternoon."

McIntosh wasn't very keen on that but said he would.

During the night when the doctor was checking on the wounded man, he said his brother had gotten backed over by a horse and tore his arm open. It was in a bad spot, and he really needed to be stitched up proper. He was wanting to know if the Colonel would allow the doctor to work on him.

The doctor told him, "I'm a doctor, I swore an oath to help all I can and cause no harm. If he's hurt and wants me to help, I don't need the okay from Colonel Adams."

So, the next morning, right after breakfast, me and Chuck were sent to get this guy's brother. We had a note for Mr. McIntosh asking to let the injured man come with us. We got there to a wall of guns. I gave the note to McIntosh, and it was easy to see he could not read it.

Chuck pipes right up, "Where's the one with the badly cut arm? Your brother firmed it up with the doctor to clean it up and fix it the best he can." A young guy came up leading a so-so horse. We told him the doctor would look at his arm if he wanted. He mounted up and we headed out, being sure to keep him between us and the armed camp.

When we got to the doctor, we just stood around to be sure this new patient caused the doctor no trouble. When the two brothers were together, the one a gunshot wound and the other a bum arm, the doctor unwrapped the arm. I never saw such a thing. It was cut badly just above the elbow. As the doctor stared at it, I stepped in for a closer look. Someone had sewed it up and they had poured hot pine pitch on the edges and stuck short pieces of string in it to cool and be stuck fast. It was my first look at backwoods, Indian style stitches. As the doctor worked on the arm, he was quiet and never said a word. He cleaned it all up and told the young man if he could keep it clean, and the stitches tight, it should heal just fine. The doctor sent the brothers on their way with a batch of something to clean both of their wounds. They rode away happy, and the doctor just shook his head.

CHAPTER 20

Family Fears

It was time to get our next setup. We went to the Colonel's tent. There were a lot of people in front of us, so we waited. When it was our turn, the Colonel introduced us to those who were there as the United States Army Snipers. He walked up, stiff legged and handed each of us a badge for our green uniform jackets. He stood in front of us and said, "I am promoting both if you to the rank of Captain."

Then he thanked us and almost shook our arms off.

We had been given two little badges to pin on our jackets.

"If I wear this little thing from them," said Chuck. "it gets me two dollars a month more pay. So, I'll wear it and, maybe, get me another to wear."

We each unceremoniously got our Sniper Badges, and both agreed to put them right on so we could start drawing $2.00 a month more pay.

The next day, a funny thing happened. It just happened to be payday and every payday I would send at least half my pay home. On this day, the postmaster had two little things for me. I did not get letters from home so was not sure what was happening.

The postmaster said, "My cousin is the postmaster in your hometown. He knows where I was and sent those two letters back with a note to try and get them back to you. It seems," he continued, "that your last two letters with money in them were sent back with a note saying there wasn't anyone living at your house to deliver the mail to. My cousin wanted to make sure to get these letters back to you."

Both letters were still sealed up and had the full amount of money in there. I was stunned and I could not figure out where they could go to be delivered, or who to ask. I was numb deep in my gut. So many questions, so many unanswered questions. The postmaster had no answers, but he promised to get his cousin on it. I felt I needed to go find my family or find out what happened to them.

That night, I lay awake wondering what could have happened. Why were the letters returned? I was sure the southern army had not gotten that far north yet. I was in fear of what could happened to Ma and Pa. I was sure they would have given all they could so as not to have bloodshed. Also, I worried about Priscila and Helen. At 15 years old, Priscila was a young woman. I got hot chills as I thought of what might have been done to her if taken against her will to an enemy army camp. I cried into my hands so as not to wake Chuck. Many things went through my mind, like my sister being raped or abused, because I knew all too well how men being away from home behave, two years for some men. With those men and her being the enemy, it was possible. I wrote about it and it was hard to even write the words raped or death. Young Helen, she would be about 12 years old now, and it would be the same fate for her. It didn't take long before I made up my mind I needed to go home and find out if I could.

As I was stuffing my things into saddlebags, Chuck found me and asked, "What do you think you are doing?"

I told him my plan to go home.

He replied, "You really think you will be allowed to take off for your own problems? If that was so, no one would be here. I know how you feel."

"How can you know how I feel?" I asked. "This is my whole family that is gone, and I'm thinking the worst for the girls. Also, Ma and Pa, and what about my brother Andy? Andy paid his dues, Pa would always say. What has happened to him? I just have to go. I am sure I have done enough for this army that Colonel Carpenter would see things my way and let me go."

But when I asked Colonel Carpenter, I found that he and Chuck had the same idea. They could not let everybody who might have lost family go home to check. Nobody let go would ever come back.

So, I was not going to be allowed to go, unless I just snuck off. With this new idea rolling around in my head, I saw that both mules were now gone. I was planning a quick trip and needed Sue.

That night, I got up to go to the trench, and right off I saw there were shadows following me everywhere. They were just not going to let me go home. I did realize the time factor was against me. We were looking at three to four months. The ache in my gut burned a hole through my heart. Now I hated the south and north because they were no better in things like this, and most of all I was hating war!

Everybody I talked to did not agree with me about going home and felt that I should not be allowed to go home on leave. I hated them. Darn Chuck, my closest friend, was trying to get me to understand that there was nothing I could do or get done by going home. I even hated him now! I hated this world and everything in it, including myself.

It was no surprise that I was taken off active sniper work, my Sharps was taken away, and Chuck worked alone. At night I was put in a tent that amounted to a holding cell without bars. One evening, as I was making my bed, four people came in. One was Colonel Carpenter, then his aide and another man who started going through my bed stuff, and the last was Chuck. I just looked at Chuck, wondering what he had done to be locked up. We stared at each other for a time.

At last Chuck asked me, "What"?

I told him I was just wondering what he did to get locked up with me.

"We're a team," he told me. "We're a team and I don't want you to end up standing in front of a firing squad. I'll hold your hand all night if that was what will keep you here alive."

After two weeks, things were back to old hat. Only one more week and I got my Sharps back and I was allowed lots of brushing time with Sue.

As I said before, that mule had more skills than any horse I ever heard of. One time, one of the hostlers came over and told me what he found out about her. I learned there were so many things I did not know how or why to use. Sue could lay down to mount, ground tie, and had different speeds of gait. She could walk on her back legs and lay down flat to hide in short cover. When we talked, the hostler said it was best right now not to talk about Sue's skills or show her off to the rest of the men. Someone could steal her in the night, or a new officer might be told he could just take her. Every officer wanted a gaited trotting horse for parading in front of the President or for other days the officer was put in front of his troops. The one new thing me and the hostlers taught her was to come to a name call or low whistle. The whistle I learned to use was made like a bird call, using a willow bark flute.

CHAPTER 21

The Veterinarian

Chuck and me had no sniper work right off, so every morning we checked our gear, and looked after our mules. We knew they could very well be our lifeline to get us away and back to one of our closed hideouts. This way we never took them to our main camp. We were sure they knew where it was. It's just riding with us they could break away from us and get to Colonel Carpenter and our supply house.

One day, after giving our mules their morning care, we were assigned to help someone. Most of the time, it was to deal with the stock. I had only heard of animal doctors, but Chuck had seen them working. With all the horses alone, it took more than the four blacksmiths we had, working all day, every day to keep their feet and legs usable. The blacksmiths needed help. The new doctors were called "Veterinarians." We had three with us to start. This included a "Head Vet" and two helpers who learned all they could, then were sent to other outfits.

Our horses and mules had a whole range of problems, from worn-down feet, to saddle sores. Some of the wagon stock had bad rubbed spots from poor fitting harnesses or a heavy load put on their necks. These top neck sores were called "pyoderma" and a bad one most of the time cannot be cured.

That's where Chuck and me came in. All the animals the vet said he could not fix were sent away to be shot. During the war, many things came up that I did not like, and remember to this day. The animals to be shot were driven, limping and dragging themselves, to a spot about ten miles south. I heard there were horses that had everything you think of wrong with them. I saw broken legs, and legs shot clean off. They had swelled up faces and jaws so bad they could not open their mouths to eat. More than one was pointed out to have a cannon hole shot clean through their skin on the top of their necks.

Now came the sad part. At the shooting spot were a row of posts. We were told to tie a horse to each post and get back over the ridge. As I jumped down, I grabbed my Sharps and started to set her up for work. Chuck just sat there looking at me. I looked back.

"You won't need that," Chuck said.

"Why?" I asked just as the first cannon shot shocked the valley.

Again, again and again the cannons fired until all the tied horses were no more. I figured out what had happened. The tied horses were being used as real live targets for the cannon crews. After three or four rounds of this slaughter, we had a hard time finding a post. The ground was soft and slippery with a fresh coat of blood and body fluids covering everything. There were small body parts, over 100, around each post, covering the trees, short brush, and trees with anything that would get caught and hang on. The blood was different. It got on anything it touched. It made the ground soft and slippery. It turned that hillside into a slop yard. I could not get the sight or smell of all this blood and stomach contents in the air, out of my mind. To this day, I have choking and gagging dreams that flash back to my mind and body the whole of what I saw that day. Try as I might, these memories do not go away or get any better even though I was put through all kinds of doctor care. When I got my last check up and was given a signed "Fit for service" result, Chuck was right there. He said we started as a team, and he had no wish to change that. It took a week or more to get even one good night's sleep, but we got through it.

CHAPTER 22

Hideouts

After I began to feel myself again, Chuck and I were sent on a two-week ramble. We were instructed to change into buckskin shirts and pants after we went northwest from Shippensburg. We worked our way west until we dropped down into Uniontown. We talked to the farmers along the way, and it seemed the only time they heard about the war was when a group of young guys went by and they were looking for a fight. Most all of these groups were fueled by corn liquor. In many of the towns there was no talk. Only the towns with railroad spur lines had any news and that news was about two months old!

In Uniontown they were real close-lipped about covert army and war things. Some said there was a small, but well supplied army down a spur line. Others played dumb or outright said, "fake." We played dumb as well. We got some traps and other gear and bought an armload of fur from a trapper. Now we looked the part.

In disguise, we poked around every rail spur. We narrowed it down to just one. It was well looked after and ended in an underground mineshaft. We never were able to get a look inside. We marked it on our map and moved on. We followed the ridgeline, spotting with our spy glasses. We worked off to the east because we had been out close to two months and were not sure how far west we were. If we got back to our base camp by the end of the month, we would be in good shape.

When we got near to camp, we heard people here and there making comments about killing all the horses and mules. Any time you left camp to the north, you could smell the stench drifting on the wind. The smell of blood still gags up in my throat.

We decided to report that things were in an uproar and changed back into our uniforms. Our riding mules were all decked out in army gear which was the red flag. We were stopped at the camp gate and were not surprised by that. The surprise came when we were surrounded by all these bad looking men with loaded rifles. When I saw them, my hand went to my revolver, on its own, and then was reaching for my Sharps when a big fist grabbed my hand and dragged me off Sue. Chuck was getting the same treatment. This big guy was standing on my back so that I could hardly breathe.

Meanwhile, leave it to Chuck to raise a fuss. He started yelling at the top of his lungs, calling them everything but a white man. Chuck was demanding to see Colonel Carpenter, or at least his personal aide.

After what seemed like an hour, we were allowed to get up and handcuffed to two close trees. I was starting to get a little twitchy by now. Ants and 'skeeters got to me and I could not swat them off my face or anyplace else. Soon we were drug into a lockup cell. It kept the bugs away, but we couldn't see if anything was being done to get Colonel Carpenter or his aide.

Later, it must have been chow call because they threw two plates of beans, one biscuit and a container of water to us. We had been on the go all day and had not eaten, so, as meager as it was, we gladly ate it.

It was just about dark when I heard the Colonel's aide talking. I wasn't sure where, but it had to be close. I could clearly hear him say, "If they are who they say they are, Colonel Carpenter will not like you roughing them up."

All of a sudden, there was the rattle of keys and the door swung open. We were free! We went right to Colonel Carpenter and gave him our report. We were sure to tell him about the train track that ended in a mineshaft. When we were finished reporting, we made our way back to our tent. We had not taken a shower or shave in a good while, but it did not bother us to flop down and sleep.

In the middle of the night, I bolted right up. I had not seen our mules or our gear since we were locked up. I reached over and shook Chuck awake and told him. He rolled right over into his boots and was off at a run with me close behind. When we got back to the front gate, the shift had changed, and the new men knew nothing. So, we were off at a run for the horse lot, but when we got to the old spot, it had been moved. Chuck and I both found a little breezeway and started cutting across it to catch the smell of a horse yard. Within a city block, we found it. Now we had to face the guys on guard duty. Of course, when we walked into the lantern light, long beards and buckskin shirt & pants, we were faced with a circle of guns again.

We gave them our best story and didn't think they bought it. They told us to sit down, back-to-back, and they dropped a lariat around both of us. They had a big pow-wow. They had been told that two guys were making the rounds around the outside of the camp. These two guys making the rounds were checking out stories about two men who came and went at all hours and rode two mules. We would have to wait until these two guys returned.

There were light streaks in the eastern sky when two half-drunks came wandering in. They were wide eyed when we jumped to our feet. One guy said he had seen us before, coming and going for two years. So, they sprung us loose and now the hunt was on for gear. Some guys went with us and we found everything in a pile, with our saddles stacked on top. Right away, I saw my gear boxes and noticed my Sharps laying on the ground next to the pile.

Then, last but not least we asked, "Where's our mules?"

They said all animals were in the lot, so our mules had to be there somewhere. We told them we kept our mules in a lot up closer to us, so we needed to find them. I was all for searching the lot, but Chuck had another plan.

"I'm not walking out in that knee deep slop yard," Chuck said. "Let's you and me go off where it's quiet and try calling them."

Instead of going into the lot, we walked down the side of the fence, away from the slop, and started calling real softly and making a low whistle. We had a half moon but big clouds drifting in made it pitch black. After two or three whistles, when a cloud went past and the moon shined down, there stood Sue. Chuck was ready to give up and started bad-mouthing his mule, calling him a long-eared knot head. But just as Chuck turned to give up, there he stood, right next to Sue.

We had no trouble getting our hands on the mules and leading them to the gate. Now we had the whole herd on our heels and needed the guard crew to hold the other animals back. We gathered our mules and gear and headed to the clearing behind the blacksmith tent. There was still a food barrel with good feed in it and a brick of hay. We fed the mules grain in the boxes, then grabbed their bridles and snapped them onto the high-line.

Back at the tent, Chuck spoke up for the first time,

"Woke up a touch worried about our gear," he said.

I told him I agreed and would give everything a good cleaning in the morning.

We woke up to a drizzling rain. After a quick bite of food, we checked the mules and set to cleaning our gear. There was nothing really bad, but we didn't want to let it slide. Just as we finished up, the Colonel's aide came calling, saying the Colonel wanted to talk to us soon.

When we got there, the maps were spread on the table, and the curtains were up. The road patrol sent word that a group of 18 to 20 southern soldiers were traveling back and forth, as if they were looking for the best route to bring a large force north. The rebels had been spotted in several places, but they had done nothing but camp overnight and move on in the morning.

The Colonel explained that our job was to hunt them down and decide who the leader was. Once we found the enemy soldiers, we had to try to take the leader and the second in command out of the fight. The Colonel hoped this would stop them, if not slow them way down. When they were stopped or slowed, we could gather our troops and capture the whole squad.

We spent a good hour studying the maps, then two field generals were called in because they both had spent lots of time in that area, escorting the sending of military records and general mail. The generals pointed out the spots they would hide out and why. Also, the area they felt would be used by the enemy to march north if coming by land. We had to agree with them because they knew the area and we had never been there and had no time to go see for ourselves.

They assembled four groups of 20 men and showed them on the map where each group would hide out to wait for Chuck and me to do our job. We set off and were lucky to be following a trail so worn down, it was almost a road. Two of the hiding places were near railroad tracks and each time our men heard the train, they could easily check it.

As we parted company with the third group, we dipped way south. Also, we were looking for a hill so we could get a better view. We had learned early on that our time spent looking through a spy glass was way better the wandering around the country and found us more to report than we found in hours and days riding.

We needed high ground, but everything was pretty flat. From everywhere we rode and everywhere we looked, the only high thing was a big old barn. It must have been 50 to 60 feet high and had a shed on the back side that was half as high. This was our only high ground for miles. We checked out the house real well and found no one inside, but there were animals in the barn. We just could not reason why there were cows and horses in the barn. Someone had to fork hay and carry a good amount of water, at least two times a day. The barn doors were locked but we looked through knotholes and could see inside. The only thing I noticed was that the horses were young stock. All of them were too young to be bred. It seemed they were kind'a hidden, so as not to be lost to the army.

Chuck and me separated and made a couple of big circles and met back outside the barn. We did find that there just wasn't any other livestock in the area. We needed to find out who the animals belonged to, and when did somebody do the chores. We each took a fistful of jerky, and an apple. Then we sat back and waited.

I woke up to a hard thump between my shoulders. I almost yelled out, not knowing right off where I was or what was happening. A gentle shove got me fully awake. Thank the Lord, Sue was keeping guard and not nodding off. She had heard, seen or smelled someone coming up the drive to the back. Knowing I was asleep, she had whacked me on the back to get me awake and going. Chuck was up too.

We right away heard somebody walking. As the person got closer, we could see it was a woman. Her lantern was turned really low and she was working her way along the rocky road, leading a horse. She stopped and pulled something from her apron pocket and offered it to a prancing colt. That was it, she was going to bridle him to get him under control and not be walking on her feet. After she had ridden our way, it took her about an hour to feed and water all the animals.

Chuck and me had talked it over, as to what we were going to do if a guy showed up. This was a lady, though. We never thought of that. When she left, I followed her back down the road about two miles. I don't even think she knew I was there, at least, she never looked back. While I followed her down the road, Chuck poked around the farm.

When I got back, he pointed out where someone had boards nailed on the side of the shed that could be used for steps to get on the roof of the shed. Well, climbing up there got us to the level of the treetops, but did not really help. If there was a campfire within the closer five miles, we could see it. Really, though, we have found as many fires by smelling the smoke, as to seeing a campfire.

Since the barn doors were locked, we would have to break in. This could be a bad deal. If we broke in, the woman would know someone was there and we would for sure lose the barn roof. Or if we went up, we would get caught on it. So, we did not want to break in. About then Chuck spotted something.

"Look here," he said.

While I had been looking the countryside over, Chuck found a small door that led us to a ladder and into the upper storage of the barn. This barn was made with big old beam framework and was over half-full of loose piled hay. We worked our way across the beams to the center of the building. This put us right below a large air vent mounted on the roof. This big vent is called a cupola. Not only did it allow hot damp air out, it also allowed a way to get onto the outside of the roof.

I heard some scrambling around and when I looked to see where Chuck was perched, he was gone. He had been able to get a hold of the hay rail and was able to pull himself up. He was telling me to come on up.

"Where did you put your gun"? I asked.

"I left it on the roof by the window we climbed through," he replied.

So, I propped mine up next to his and started to pull myself up. When we got one of the shutters open in the cupola, we were able to walk out onto the big roof. It was like being on top of a ship which was belly-up in the water. Up so high in the dark, we were afraid to wander too close to the area of the roof where it curved over the edge and down into the blackness. Instead, we stayed put and looked out to the countryside.

We saw two places where there were lots of small fires, like we saw at any camp. In our northern camps, we had a fire for every six to eight tents. Most of the time we did not even have a coffee pot, just a place to sit and talk to everyone. In our camp we were always pestered by the new guys and their questions as to what we did. It was easy to see we weren't "flat shoe" solders. We were gone sometime in the two-month time frame. We were never covered in mud from crawling in ditches to hide, get away or get shot. When talk came up, we said nothing and if someone did not tell the new guys to knock it off, we just went to our tent.

After a time, we left the barn. As we left, we figured it would be a good time to check out the new camp we had seen from the barn roof. As we thought, it was a small camp, probably a group of forward scouts looking for the best place to hop across to Pennsylvania. They had a fear of Maryland believers who were wishy-washy on the issue of moving slow. These wishy-washy guys did not want to move in and set up a large supply dump and have it overrun and lose everything.

In the dark, we were able to wander right into the camp and have a cup of coffee at an empty campfire, and Chuck even used their trench. With two men to a tent, they did not have a camp of two hundred men. They did have a couple of large tents set up. We figured one was a cook and supply tent and the other was not really a tent, but a stack of wooden boxes and crates, covered with sail cloth to stay dry. To look at it, your first thought was supplies going north. The only thing I saw was a real low, or short, was their supply of horses. The few oxen on hand were old and worn down. They were all headed for the stew pot, most before winter.

We saw all that we needed to see and were taking our leave, when somewhere out in darkness, a voice said, "Halt, who goes there?"

This was something I feared all the time, being caught in an enemy camp, and now it was happening. We had talked about it some and decided if it was at night, like now, we had a chance to get away. Our plan was to just bolt away into the night. Each of us going in a different direction and zig-zagging our way out of the camp. Somehow, we'd get back to our mules, and if lucky, we'd head for the main east-west trail or road.

Well, it turns out that this night guard was not too fired up or even awake. He didn't fire a shot, and I think he never even yelled again. But I was not going to stand around and give him pointers. Chuck ran and so did I. When I got to the edge of camp, it was evident there was no one giving us chase.

In the dark, I drifted around until I found the little creek where the willow brush was really thick and we had left the mules. By tying them in the thick leafy brush, they had little trouble with 'skeeters getting them. Without anything bothering them, they could stand quiet for a good while. No one would ever hear them stomping their feet to rid themselves of night bugs and 'skeeters.

I stepped in close to Sue, talking low and softly. I ran my hands over her to chase away any hanging-on bugs and making sure there were no little sticks or tall grass stems caught in her tack straps. With everything checking out okay, I drew the girth up tight and got ready to mount up and go.

I was just moving slow so Chuck would have a chance to get here and get ready to ride. I had slipped up on Sue real quiet and turned toward the trail on high ground. I could direct Sue with my knees and keep going slow so there was no need for me dragging on her bit. We got out onto the trail and Sue paused only slightly, waiting for my cue to go left or right. I bumped her with my right knee, and she knew to go left down the trail.

Sue made maybe two full steps and drew up short, drifting off to the right. At that minute, out of the darkness, Old Bob's head bumped me in the shoulder. This was a big surprise, but I knew it had to be Chuck or Old Bob. Otherwise, Sue would not have let either of them get that close without dropping back or farther off trail to the right.

Not a word was spoken, just a wave and point beyond me and Chuck, and we knew where we were going. We let the mules step out for about ten miles, and into a tight grove of thorn bushes and willow. We had stopped in here many times and had a trail into the grove cut from the backside. We always pulled a cut branch over and into the trail. This way we could tell right off if anyone was about or just stopped by. The bush was where we had left it, so we felt okay going in.

At these times, I was the cautious one, and Chuck just always said "Looks good to me" and rode right in. I was okay without leading this time. My family had lost enough to this war, and I was in no hurry to add any more.

CHAPTER 23

The Creek

Hidden in our grove, we ate cold beans and jerky while we figured out locations of the enemy campfires. It stood to reason with us that farmers would be burning fires to cook and eat inside some sort of shelter. Most farmers had log walls built up about four feet so they could have fires and not be seen from the ground level. Only people like us and probably soldiers, wandering the countryside for one reason or the other, would have an open campfire. We had the fires in our heads and would check them in the morning.

At dawn, we were moving down and kicked up a little dirt as we were headed east, when Sue stopped short and tried to back up. At the same time that she stopped, I noticed the smell of smoke and fried bacon drifting in the air. Sue side-stepped over to the ditch and then she scrambled up the bank. Chuck and Bob followed. Now we were above the brush enough to see a well-laid out camp.

From this high ground, I could count about a dozen tents that would sleep four men easily. One well-hidden tent was probably for cooking and supplies. There were only four horses to be seen, so we figured the rebels were out for the day and night, and not anyone around. However, we were wrong. We would come to find out there were four people there, a cook, one guard on duty, and two sleeping in plain sight, probably from all-night guard duty.

We were in our buckskins, so we just rode right in. The guards all jumped up but never pointed any guns. The cook seemed in charge, or at least, he was the one doing the talking.

"Hey, what's going on?" he yelled.

Chuck said we were just going back to where we left our pack of pelts and smelled your fire.

"We are headed to Baltimore to turn them in to our store house," Chuck continued. "We are hauling pelts from about ten traps from the upper Midwest area and trying to get better prices then we're getting in Pittsburgh,"

Hearing Chuck's explanation, the cook seemed relaxed, and he asked us, "Eat yet? No? Sit down for a bite."

We did not see anybody hiding from view, so we felt safe. He told us we could tie our mules and give them some feed also. Then he asked if we knew anything about this country.

"Not much," Chuck answered. "Only been by here two other times."

We swapped pleasantries but guessed things could change when we started to leave. The coffee was good, the bacon was better, wrapped around two fresh biscuits. It was hard to turn away. When we said we did not want to wear out our welcome and must be moving on, to our surprise he told us to get a handful of biscuits and a fist full of bacon to take with us. So, we got away as easily as we got in. We never heard a word of what they were doing in the area, and they never questioned us anymore. It seemed quite odd to us.

Leaving the rebel camp, we rode east at a good clip, then after a couple of miles there was a rock seam running across the road. It was wide enough that a rider could turn at a sharp angle and get off the road and not leave any tracks. So that's what we did, cut to the north and went on a short ride back to the west. We found ourselves overlooking the road and the little hollow where the camp was. We staked out there in the sun and ate our bacon and biscuits while keeping an eye on our new friends. They never went anywhere, and nobody came for the hour that we watched them. So, still not knowing what to think, we pushed on for a couple of hours to get ourselves well past them, and close to our own base camp.

We came riding in just at the end of chow. We rode right up to the front of mess hall, chow tent, so we would be sure to get fed. Then we sent word to Colonel Carpenter that we were in and needed to talk. Everything worked out just as we planned. Colonel Carpenter's aide spotted us right off and took charge. We kept our long guns and shoulder bags while he sent our mules to their own tie outs.

At the Colonel's tent, we were pushed into the back room to a worktable. Good coffee, fresh biscuits and well-done pork hocks, came on a steaming platter. We'd already eaten a bit, but more was alight with us. Halfway through eating, we were told they would have the tent flap up shortly.

When the flap was up, we had the maps in front of us again and we showed everywhere we had seen campfires from the barn roof, and where the camp we went into was. No one could believe the enemy was camped right under their noses. No one ever saw a trail going off to the little valley. Watching that camp was put in someone else's hands and we were put into service down the road even farther. We were to work our way south and find the main rebel camp, or camps. It was felt they had around 15 men getting ready to push north. If we could find those men, it would sure help. It was talked about that someone in our northern ranks might have helped the rebels hide their camp, but nothing came of that idea.

We had a job set up for us but no real orders of when to pull out, so I said, "The mules need a good feed and rest, and I have not shot my Sharps for close to two weeks. I think we should lay up one more day to rest them and take the day to shoot our guns."

So, that is what we did. Then we took another good long look at the maps.

Next day, we slipped out around midnight. The mules were fresh and stepped right along. When we got to the area of the hidden camp, we slowed to a walk so their footfalls would not be so loud. I was not able to hear or see or even smell anything that said the camp was still there. We were told the rebels had been traveling in the river to hide their camp, but they were behind us now. We needed to get to the first well-worn trail, or road heading south.

Just at dawn, we found the road we were looking for. I thought leaving at midnight was a little early but if we hadn't got an early start we would not have had as good luck traveling as we did. We only came across one group of wagons which seemed headed west and they were pulled by oxen. The oxen were all tied out in a field next to the road and kept in place by a picket pin and a chain that had one end hooked to a ring in their nose. The oxen were picketed with a short metal pin, less than two feet long. If a stick had been used and an ox got to scratching its head, it could work the wooden stake out and wander off. I knew that most experienced ox people trained the animals to stay all the time. If they drove a stake in real deep and cut the top off, the oxen would learn they could not get lose and would not try. It's a rather funny thought that, although they seemed to be tied fast to the picket pins, if they flipped the chain over their necks, they would lift it right out of the ground. As for the wagons, they were all parked alongside the road. The camps were there too. They had saddle horses in a small rope corral.

We never did more than wave as we went by. Everyone we met really liked our mules and the way they gaited. We would be hard-pressed to go through a town fast but that would draw attention to ourselves. Our mules were the best gaited that I ever saw and, being well fed and brushed, they caught everyone's eye.

That day, we had put six medium to hard miles on the mules, so we were looking for somewhere to lay up and rest them. Also, we could eat our pork which the cook sent with us. We headed for a brushy creekbank. Not finding any tracks there, or anything else that told us somebody was around, we dropped below the bushy bank and slid off.

First things first, we made another trip around on foot just to be sure we were alone. Then we led the mules into the thickest part so they would not be pestered by flies. Also, they were out of sight. We ate quick and slipped in by the mules and got a little nap.

After a while, I was woken by Sue pushing me with her nose. As soon as I was awake, I could tell there was trouble. I could hear voices, and none of them was Chuck. There seemed to be three boys playing in the creek. That, itself, was okay because we were back away from the creek. The problem was their dog. The dog was aware there was something in the bush and he was sniffing close to us. We were just about to be found, when one boy yelled, "Boomer," get over here!"

Then, just like that, the dog turned tail and left. I'm not sure what we would have done if the dog hadn't been called back. I was not up to shooting kids. Hell, I did not want to shoot men who were shooting at me at close range. My background had steered me away from all the killing, the war had steered me back. Thank God I was a sniper, so I didn't have to face most of my targets close up. As a whole, I have only shot four men at close range.

We wanted to ride off as soon as the boys and their nosy dog were down the creek some. In the heat of the day, we were headed south, on a dusty road filled with farmers going to the market. We just could not find any high ground to spy on anyone. We found a grove of trees that had two tall pines. We made a small day camp and waited until dark. We each climbed a tree and didn't see anything but two small fires. It could have been anyone, but for sure, it was not a southern army camp.

We spent most of the night up there. The big limbs were easy to sit on. In fact, falling asleep was the real worry. A fall from that high would break something most likely, like my neck!

On the next day, we pushed further south. We could have easily thought the war had left and gone home, for all it seemed to touch in this area. We found another grove of trees and we thought it would be as good as last night's place, but no deal! When we got there, we saw a farmhouse and an outbuilding, so no place there to hide. As we crossed behind the farm, Chuck said, "It's full of saddle horses. What are they doing there?"

Well, we had no idea, there were no men about or wagons anywhere. We decided we would spy on them in the morning. Now was the time to find a hide-out and try to do spying of some kind.

The next morning, we heard cannons in the distance. So, we went back to the farm to check that out. We weren't even close when a column of two-by-two troops swung out onto the road and headed north. We avoided them and snuck into the farm and found nobody there and the house all closed up. The barn looked like it could hold about 40 horses stabled there and probably the men slept in the hay loft. We never knew if they were north or south troops, because they were gone and, like us, on patrol. We were sure to mark it well on our maps and headed toward the sound of cannon fire.

All this time the enemy was still in the area west of Fredericksburg, Virginia. I just could not see them still bogged down there. So, we slipped in real close. Our luck had us wearing buckskins and moccasins. We could always claim to be trappers, trying to meet up with the main group and then on to Baltimore. Soon, we found the cannons and had to wait until those men shooting them went back to camp so we could follow them.

Turns out, they had a camp along a river with high banks. They were okay as long as it was not raining, causing a flood. They had the same trench dug as well as all camps did. They were so spread out that they had three trenches that I could find.

Well, there was no high ground, or anywhere for us to hide. We were just sitting on the riverbank when one of the guards spotted us. We were hauled into camp. We were not treated that well. They fed us beans and coffee and asked all the usual questions. We were still the old trappers heading for Baltimore. We could see about 300 men. They were short on powder and shot, just laying up waiting for a supply train to bring them something soon.

I asked, "If you are low on powder, it must be short for others."

Right away someone said yes, that another camp ten miles or so east near the Rappahannock River Bridge was also short.

Another guy said, "Our powder got wet and we're having to load heavy to get anything out of it."

These rebels were talkers, but they got a little upset when we would not tie our mules up and come into their mess tent. I was sure they wanted us out of the way to go through our stuff and the new map was in there.

One old guy who was the cook's helper, said, "Don't blame you for not wanting to go inside that old tent. Sit on that log and I'll fetch a cup and plate for you."

We sat down then and ate with a couple hundred-foot troops staring at us. We tried to look small and at the same time, take it all in. There were a lot of men doing little or nothing while waiting for a supply train to come to their aid.

I had all the coffee and beans I could eat and drink and started checking things to get going. I was ready to ride when I caught Chuck's eye, and he stood up. Right away someone said, "What's the hurry?"

We just said that we needed to get going and try to be there before dark. Chuck checked his stuff and all seemed well. We still carried a fishing pole in with our Sharps to hide them. All of a sudden, the cook's helper ran up and gave a feed sack to us.

Later, as we rode along, we found fresh donuts and enough feed and side meats to keep us eating for a couple of days. We were grateful for the food but just a little upset that we left and never got one shot off. We decided to try swinging back on our way home. Then set up a shooting spot and be able to rest the mules. On our return trip, at dark as the rebels turned their tired horses int0 the barn, we could shoot from a distance and outrun them in the night.

We found their other camp really easy. There were twice as many rebels there, but they were doing very little in the ways of war. They seemed to be just holding their spot. After two days of snooping around their camp, we did not see any reason to just be sitting there. We left and went upriver about four miles and swam the mules across. We found a spot for the night and got out of our wet buckskins. I woke up to mosquitoes eating me up and found Chuck the same. He would not complain but his face was all red welts. We rode downriver by way of the road close by. We had ridden all around camps that were protected by southern cannon fire.

CHAPTER 24

Chow Call

It was showing morning light when we finally got back to our northern field camp. We rode right up the road and through the main gate. Both guys on guard knew us, so getting back in was no problem. We felt we had a few liberties that other guys didn't get. Once on, we rode right up to the back of the mess tent. Chuck had to tie Bob up, but Sue would stand "ground tied." So, I parked Sue under a shade tree where she would not get tripped up in tent ropes, then Chuck tied Bob to her. We were sure they would be right there when we came back, as long as no one had led them away.

One more of our liberties was to sit at the cook's table in the backroom and have our meal brought to us. We always got fresh coffee and warm food, no matter what meal we were eating. As we ate, Colonel Carpenter was told we were back. His aide came and told us to sit tight until we were called. After two or three cups of coffee, we wandered over to Colonel Carpenter's tent. Another liberty to come without being called. After we arrived, field generals were called, and the sides were tied up. Everybody was served coffee again and introduced to us.

Once again, the Colonel's aide brought the maps out and we were able to point out everything we saw. Everyone was sure the south was going to jump the line and get into Southern Pennsylvania. We helped show them where to set up blockade spots along the road and all railway tracks. Chuck pointed out it was going to be hard to stop a moving train, and he felt something else needed to be put into the mix.

Colonel Carpenter said, "If you got something in mind, we would be happy to here it."

So, Chuck started telling his plan.

He said, "We need to destroy every railroad bridge from here where we sit, clear back east to the Atlantic shore."

That idea was talked around but burning bridges was put on hold. It was agreed that six to eight sections of rail be removed from the bridges and taken away. That way, the enemy would be stopped there until new rails were found and replaced in the bridge deck. Then our side would be able to put the bridge back in service if we needed it in the future.

We all agreed and Chuck and me were told to get a shave and shower and check back after noon meal. At this point Chuck jumped up and yelled, "Hey, where are you going with my mule?"

That really surprised everyone. Over the table he went, tripping on a tent rope and slipping in the mud. I ran after my partner. Just our luck, one of the blacksmith helpers was leading a string of horses over to the turn out and heard and saw everything. He knew how we felt about our mules, and knew something was up with Chuck and me up on the hill, and another rider coming down from the tent area leading Chuck's mule. So, the helper just slowed his string down to an amble and blocked the way. Another guard from the front gate was on day rest, headed to the trench and just wandered into the road, as well. When Bob got close, that guard just grabbed the reins from the rider and the "runaway" was over.

As for the thief, the leader of the guards had him by the scuff of the neck and on the ground by the time Chuck and I got there. Chuck ran right up to him and was going to thump him real good, all the while, yelling, "Horse thief! We hang our horse thieves!"

All at once Chuck realized he knew the man. About then, everybody was yelling and looking for somewhere to start a fight. Well, the fight never happened, but Chuck got to drag him away and blow some steam off.

"You know Bob's my mule! Why would you steal him?" Chuck yelled. Well, the poor guy never got a chance to say anything.

Before anything else happened, Colonel Carpenter shouldered his way to the front and took charge.

"Listen up here," the Colonel ordered.

All talking stopped and everyone did listen. Colonel Carpenter ordered everyone to return to their duties and ordered that the young man be brought to his tent. Chuck and I followed.

When we all arrived at the Colonel's tent, we went inside, and the tent flap was closed.

"What are you doing, son?" the Colonel asked. "I think I know you," he continued.

The young man just shook his head and said, "Yes, sir." All this time he had a death grip on a shoulder bag.

"What's in the bag son?" the Colonel asked.

The young man answered, "Not real sure, sir, but mostly letters and documents headed to Washington and the war department at the Capitol.

The Colonel said, "You steal a horse, then a mail deposit and not sure what's in it?"

The young man told the Colonel, he didn't steal it, that he was told to take it. He continued, "I take one every two or three days to the train station."

"You're a dispatch rider"? the Colonel asked.

The young man replied, "Well, sir, I guess kind of. Every day or two the camp dispatch office sends me somewhere with a bag of stuff bound for somewhere."

The Colonel said something to his aide, and he ducked out of the tent. The Colonel asked him why he needed the mule, and he said that he was told to do it.

"It's getting harder and harder to believe your story," the Colonel said. "You have a mail dispatch pouch and were told to take the mule. One would not think you would try to get away on a mule."

About then, the tent flap swung open and in stepped a bald-headed officer with sergeant strips on his arm. First thing he said to our young horse thief was, "What are you doing still here? I told you to get to the train."

The young man started to tell the sergeant how he was going and following the direct roads and was stopped while trying to get out the front gate.

Colonel Carpenter interrupted asked the sergeant if the young man worked for him and the sergeant, who was the camp postmaster, replied, "Why yes, sir. He's my best rider."

The Colonel told the sergeant to check the bag and if it's right, to send the young man on his way.

All was okay and he was sent on his way. He was given a pay voucher and told to finish his delivery.

As things were unfolded, the postmaster sent a delivery rider every other day to the railroad depot to pass a packet of papers to Washington. By sending a rider every other day and not telling the contents, no one ever knew if there was important paperwork. That day it was a packet of important stuff. The postmaster told the young man to jump on the first horse he saw and get to the depot in a hurry to get it on the east-bound express for the Capitol.

When he rushed out of the postmaster's tent, there stood Bob. Being a fairly good judge of horses, he could tell Bob was no wagon mule. Standing there all saddled up, it was just about all he needed to get a good ride and not have to go to the horse lot and catch his own and sign it out.

At last, he was put on another horse, and we kept Bob. It was all aboveboard, and the young man was following orders, and not just stealing a horse. I tried to ease Chuck's mind by telling him "No harm, no foul" and that he should be proud that Bob was praised by someone else as being a good animal and would be good service for needing a good rider. Chuck was not convinced.

Anyhow, we took Bob and Sue to their private tie outs, cleaned them up and rubbed them down. When we finished with that, we had time for a couple of hours nap before chow call. We never heard any chow call, so to speak, but everyone was drifting that way, so we got up and headed that way. We thought we were kind'a first but it was easy to see there were more than a hundred ahead of us, and two or three hundred behind us. Chuck said what I was thinking, "Where did these people all come from?"

As we ate, we talked it over with another officer and he was willing to say too much. By way of him, we learned we were building up troops to form a front line on the western side. We were hoping to push the enemy back to the east as they were pushing north. He said we had way more troops in the central area and wanted to meet them head on there. The camp was gearing up for a move at the end of the month.

After that, Chuck and I went out every chance we got with the group put in charge of finding a new stop. It seemed like anywhere east of the first set of hills would do. They just needed to find a spot that had grass for our horses, and enough water for everybody. They had many to choose from, so we left it to them. We got stocked up and drifted south to find the rebel's main front line. It was not hard to find. We just watched the skies for smoke and listened for cannon fire. If we were straight out from them when fired, the cannon ball never hit us, but the sound came in a rush.

The rebels seemed to be balled up just north of the Fredericksburg, Virginia, area. They were either having a hard time gaining ground from there or they were setting up for a move. Chuck and I both thought they were camped there a long time. We pushed a clearing at the Rappahannock Bridge. It was a trip to tie up our mules after about two weeks of moving all we could manage.

At this point, we walked our way back, past all easy to remember places we had already been. We were able to do our work as we made our way back. It was plain to see the enemy was planning a big move, and it looked like it would be by rail. Our trip back was rather uneventful. We made our presence known as snipers and got about two apiece each day. We were instructed to work on the enemy's horses and mules as well. Well, neither Chuck nor myself had much in the way of good thoughts about shooting their stock. We figured they would not be shooting back, and someone would have to feed and care for them, so leaving the animals alive we were really taking one man out of the fight, since someone had to do it.

On what we thought would be our last night out, we were talking about where the new Union camp would be. I heard the name Big Pool and Chuck heard Big Spring. Both were a mile or two north of the mountain road we had been using. Anyway, it wouldn't be really hard to find. We could find them at dark by the smoke of their fire for cooking. Also, the smell of the horses' yard and the "ditch." The smell of the ditch used as the latrine was a smell that drifted on the wind and gave away the direction of any camp, new or old.

Chapter 25

Messengers

We rode into camp again while everyone was at the mess tent. We tied our mules up and got in line. We were talked to by the old camp crew, but the new recruits who did not know us gave our buckskins a looking over. They thought we were just drifters, freeloading a meal.

We were sitting cross-legged in front of our mules, finishing up our meal, when the camp aide came up. He pointed out the new location of our tent, but there was no brush patch to tie the mules to. We had no problem ground tying them but for sure could not leave them standing in the open.

Chuck asked, "Who do you think is staying in that big wall tent?"

That's when I took a good look at this 10 x 10 walled tent, set up out of line, and not real far from us. Right away, here came the aide again. We were to report as always. At this point he herded our mules over to a spry old chap who took them straight inside the old tent.

"That's a fix for your mules out of any rain, or to be seen," the Colonel's aid told us. "It has a hay manger setup and a rail for your gear."

We had our meeting and told the Colonel and the others everything we found out. It seemed like everyone else had the same idea. The enemy was bunching up their focus for a drive through Maryland and into southern Pennsylvania. The problem we all had was that we did not know if they were going to march double-time or commandeer a train to take them.

After that meeting, Chuck and I had a talk. We had been talking for the last couple of months about how this war was going. We both had been there for close to two and half years. All this time the south had been able to withstand a Union surge at Richmond and still draw their focus north to the Maryland line. The rebels felt Maryland was on their side and did not want to wage heavy war on its land. A ground war really tore up things. Most every building would be lost, and all the livestock would be stolen and eaten. If the farmer and his family gave them any trouble, they were just killed, too many times to tell. Most of the time, though, the wives and girls were raped to death. The men and boys were shot. The first time I ever heard the name of the town, Gettysburg, was in a meeting where we had to decide to try and get the enemy to an area about two miles west of there. We were going to try to set up a loose front that would funnel them to Gettysburg. I guess it worked because that's where the rebels ended up.

At this time, we more or less stopped our sniper work and now just rode up and down the outer fringes, and reported to our Colonel on where the rebels were and how well they were dug in. Using this information, added to what the Colonel already had, our side was able to set up blocking forces. Those men came in full force, in wagons, by horse, by foot and some even by train with their large depot of supplies. We set up on a south facing hilltop. We had thousands of troops and too many cannons to count quickly. This coming fight was set to be the showdown.

When the shooting started, the powder smoke just hung in the air, burning your eyes and throat. Once your ears started to ring, they never stopped. Both sides responded with cannon fire and troop rifles. The north had the advantage with more cannons and not having to worry about running out of powder and ball.

Chuck and me were now messengers. We took orders from the company commanders and took results back. Someone took note of the fact there was a road ditch and split rail fencing near the bottom of the long slope. Using these as markers, any time a southern unit made a move to gain ground by advancing to the fence, all cannons in the area would fire at them. For some reason, the rebels did not see how many troops they were losing by doing this same thing over and over again.

Every afternoon, the firing stopped and both sides would walk the fields, looking for any of their men who looked wounded. These men were taken to one of the medical tents. At these tents a new war was waging. There were way too any men, north and south both, only looked forward to the removal of an arm or leg. Most were done without anything for the pain except a leather strap put in their mouth to bite on. On into the night it went. After a couple of days like this, Chuck and I headed out to get away from the screaming men.

One morning, we saw a wagon loaded with the cut-off arms and legs to be dealt with in a mass grave that was dug along the order of our "trench" but being four or five feet deep. As dirt was dug out ahead, it was used to cover behind. So, there was always an open ditch. Our side had gotten into the habit of sending a body home if we had all the information needed to be sent to the right person in the right place. Without this information, the body could end up somewheres else.

The pace of the war picked up. Chuck and me were pushed to find our supply trains as well as the enemy's. If we could intercept a shipment of theirs and get it routed to our depots, everyone would be in high spirits. We would continue our work, but it was not as intense as it was in the past years. Mostly we were shooting shipping agents and whoever else was guarding a shipment or its delivery.

Each morning, we picked up our fresh water and two sandwiches that were handed out in the dark before troops left for the firing line. We now ate the same as everyone else. No more backroom tables for us. We were lucky to get back in time to get a serving of fried ham and beans. It wasn't as good as we ate in the past, but we were eating.

You're talking about feeding somewhere in the area of twenty thousand men, two meals a day, and that was a real task. Each division of men were assigned a mess tent. They marked every tent with a flag so men could find their tent every day. When they had to move the chow tent, the troops would come in off the firing line, in the dark, and hunt up their tent. It went way into the night to get everyone fed, and the next day's meal started.

As the mud and mines got worse, we would move to higher ground. This would bring us closer to the front line. Chuck said he felt we were within "two miles" of the cannon lines.

The ground would shake as they sent round after round from the big guns. The north had two cannon sizes, and one was the big 12-pounder. They would tear anything they hit apart. Anything, a house, a person, a horse, or whatever. It would be kindling wood if it was a building. If it was a person, well, there would only be mostly blood and scraps of the clothing they wore. A mule suffered the same fate. It would completely disembowel them with lots of blood, hide and the big bones left behind if they could be found.

A man or horse was spread around so bad, it was one of the reasons the habit of burying in mass graves was used. A lot of the bodies only had a few things left to identify who they were. A lot of times they would gather around after chow lines were done and ask everyone if all their buddies were accounted for. As a group they would backtrack where a missing man was last seen, or who he was with. Everyone would go back to the battle ground with lanterns to look for anything they could put an identifier to. Something that had their name on it, like a coat or shields on a belt knife or grip of a gun. This was what many were found by. As we came with our lanterns, we could see southern soldiers working side-by-side with northern troops doing the same thing. I never saw any conflict during our searches.

CHAPTER 26

The Dead and Wounded

One dark night, while searching for dead and wounded, I came across a round circle on the ground and its surface was all a-twinkle. Little beads of light reflected back from our lantern. I knelt down for a clear look and touched it with my finger. The whole surface was molded together but broke easily with my finger touch. I found it was a puddle of blood, and man or beast, I did not know. I was taken aback, especially when I took a quick look and saw that the whole field was like this puddle. Nearby trees were also aglow. Blood and bits of tissue hung from the branches like bulbs on a Christmas tree, except these ornaments were all red tinted from blood and body parts.

The overwhelming smell was the ruptured stomach of a horse or man. We did not see the victims, but we could smell them and knew the killing happened 10 to 20 feet towards the cannons on the hill.

I had spent a farm life growing up where we killed four or five hogs a year and two or three beef cows. Our family used that meat and even gave some to needy family members. I did not think I would be overtaken by this smell of battlefield death. I was just so glad I did not see the blood and guts in the daylight. The darkness helped but not all of the dead could be hauled away by the time to start the cannons again. In the daylight, some of the men had to climb over piles of dead men to fight. Some even used the bodies as shields to hide behind.

As the war went on, we seemed to be able to gather our dead and wounded much quicker. One of our men, who was missing a leg, said after he was shot by a southern cannon, he laid near a pile of bodies. The smell and flies were overwhelming. At one point, the buzzing of the flies filled his ears and drowned out the war. As most of the wounded would say, they had magots in their wounds, but in their own way, those magot were the reason they lived to go home. The magots ate only the dead flesh. This kept the wounds much easier to clean and keep infections from spreading.

Near the end of March, we kept hearing talk that war was going to end soon. Nobody could say where they heard that, but the whole camp had the same story. No sooner had we heard those stories than another drive by the south was down. The rebels just kept thinking they had more men than we had cannon balls. They would climb over a pile of dead bodies, to be met by a 12-pound cannon ball that sent them on their last march. It was over for them.

On March 31st, we were told it was not necessary to take a full kit of shells for whatever gun was being used. In late afternoon, many men returned saying they never fired a shot all day. Chuck and I were sent out to be sure the enemy was not trying to flank us. We found nothing and rode back into camp on April 1, 1865. We were greeted with cheers from everyone, saying the south had enough. This war was over!

As usual, Chuck called for attention and got a large group to listen to him.

"Do you all know what day it is?" Chuck asked. "It's April Fool's Day. Don't take this for real until your commander tells you so."

As it happened, no one was ordered to the field to fight. Instead, everybody went looking for the wounded who had not had any treatment yet from either the north or south troops. Two large flatbed wagons went around to gather the dead, and they filled quickly. We found wounded men covered by mangled bodies of dead men and horses, trapped by the massive weight. By the time they were dragged out, those men were nearly out of their heads.

Well, turns out the story going around was true. The south had enough. The war was over. Chuck and me got our area cleaned up and all set to turn in our gear, but nobody never asked for anything.

On April 9, 1865, Ulysses S. Grant, from the north, and Robert E. Lee, from the south, signed the papers that made the war over official. They did this at Appomattox Court House in Virginia. So many of us were numb. Was this real?

I asked Chuck and he said we had best muster out so they can't claim us as AWOL. We loaded everything on our mules and headed to the paymaster. I asked what we were to do with our stuff and he said "Just take it, you earned it." Chuck and me rode a few miles and then parted company. He was going back south, and I was heading for our home in lower Pennsylvania near York. All that time before I never knew that he was a southern boy who came north to fight against the south.

It was a long trip towards home. When I got closer, I saw more and many fires and houses burnt down. As I rode up the last stretch of road, I could see that all our rail fencing and the outbuildings were gone. The livestock was gone too. The only building left was the house. It might have been tried, but being mostly stone, there was no reason to try to burn it. I went from room to room, and just a mess remained. It looked like someone had been using an upstairs closet as the outhouse. When I got to my old room, there was old straw piled in the closet. I dug it out, just needing to see what was under that pile. I got it cleared out and only found a box in the corner that held my well-oiled boots and spats. These were the only things I found to save. The kitchen was gutted out and fires had been started in the main downstairs rooms. Destruction every place but no people anyplace.

Well, I searched the whole farm for any clues or new graves to tell me what happened to my family. I asked around but none of the old farmers in the area knew anything. Just that one day someone told them my family was gone.

Returning to the farm, I found an old bucket of paint in the pile of ashes. I used that paint to write on the outside of the house wall, telling my family that I was alive and well. I told them to keep in contact with local law. I would send a telegraph to everyone in a while. Until then, I was going to head west, to get as far away from war as I could. I put on my good boots, rolled up a bedroll and coffee pot and pan in the saddle bag and stepped up on Sue. Without telling her, the clever mule went west. I needed to get away from this war-torn area.

AFTERWORD

This war seemed to have cost me my whole family. The only things I was sure of had to do with my brothers. Walt was missing. Most likely buried in the mass graves of men at Fort Sumter. Andy had come home without his left arm, and I don't know Andrew's fate. As for the rest of my family, as of now, everyone was missing from our burnt-out farm.

www.ingramcontent.com/pod-product-compliance
Lightning Source LLC
Chambersburg PA
CBHW070047260626
47159CB00005B/2140